COPS & GOD

BROTHERS & SISTERS IN BLUE

LIEUTENANT FRANKLIN PHILIP

WESTBOW
PRESS®
A DIVISION OF THOMAS NELSON
& ZONDERVAN

WestBow Press books may be ordered through booksellers or by contacting:

WestBow Press
A Division of Thomas Nelson & Zondervan
1663 Liberty Drive
Bloomington, IN 47403
www.westbowpress.com
844-714-3454

ISBN: 978-1-6642-0301-3 (sc)
ISBN: 978-1-6642-0300-6 (hc)
ISBN: 978-1-6642-0302-0 (e)

Library of Congress Control Number: 2020916028

Print information available on the last page.

WestBow Press rev. date: 9/11/2020

Before I formed thee in the belly I knew thee; and before thou camest forth out of the womb I sanctified thee, and I ordained thee a prophet unto the nations.

—Jeremiah 1:5

There is a friend that sticketh closer than a brother.

—Proverbs 18:24

CONTENTS

FROM THE LIEUTENANT

After writing a book about *Cops & God* in 1984, little did I know the impact it would have on all its readers, especially cops.

After receiving requests from 1984 to 2010 to republish the book, I decided to expand its content and republish it. Incredibly, I abandoned the idea.

As I traveled the nation I would from time to time meet cops and other law enforcement personnel who would ask me if I was the cop who wrote *Cops & God*.

When I acknowledged that I was the author, they would tell me how the book changed their lives and led them to a closer relationship with Christ.

Indeed, I was pleased with hearing these stories and thanked God for using me to help cops cope with the many challenges they face every day they put the uniform on.

The more I got around the country in 2019 and 2020, the more cops I encountered (retired and active) who would bring up my original *Cops & God* book. In my view, all these encounters were not coincidences. I concluded that they were divine appointments.

As you read this book, you will learn that one of many ways a person can see their faith grow is by listening to the testimonies left behind by those who walked this earth during the time of Jesus and by hearing the voices of those individuals who are walking that same road today.

You will read in this book real life testimonies from people like you, about God's power, answered prayer, and much more.

The Bible tells us that "faith cometh by hearing, and hearing by the word of God" (Romans 10:17).

Cops & God reveals how faith in God through the power of prayer can lead you to a lifelong solid relationship with Jesus Christ, answered prayer, and most importantly, (if you are a cop) mold you into a very effective ambassador from the courts of heaven.

During my career as a cop I always found my strength in a strong unshakeable relationship with Jesus Christ.

This is not to say that I am different from anyone else. I am not. Quite often, I remember these words: "For all have sinned, and come short of the glory of God" (Romans 3:23).

Like all humans, I mess up from time to time. But when I do mess up, I know enough to ask God to forgive me, and He does! Hence, once I recognized that I am a sinner, saved only by the grace of God, I confessed to Him all my past sins, and He forgave me.

> If we confess our sins, he is faithful and just to forgive us our sins, and to cleanse us from all unrighteousness. (1 John 1:9)

Hundreds of cops have asked me where I learned about Christ and how my faith grew strong over the years. I told them that I did not attend a Bible school, nor did I see the earth shake, a mountain move, or some visible act of God take place. But what I did see is the silent and sure moving of the Holy Spirit in my life since the day I decided to accept Jesus Christ as my Savior.—Lt. Franklin Philip

PART 1

THE BEGINNING

DISPATCH 1

FURY AND FIRE

The sorrows of hell compassed me about:
the snares of death prevented me.
—Psalm 18:5

VP and CC were the first cops to respond to the call: civil disturbance at the corner of L Avenue and Fourteenth Street.

More than one hundred residents in this low-income housing area were milling about at the scene of the crime. It was the summer of 1974—a sultry July evening in the inner city. Heat and poverty are a combustive mixture. Tempers flare easily. Petty irritations grow into eruptions of violence.

Both cops rushed through the mob. The glare of their radio car's red lights flashed through the oppressive darkness. A man's voice challenged them. "What are you doing here?" VP turned in his direction, but his was a voice without a face, lost in a sea of angry scowls and hateful jeers. The hate-filled faces cursed and taunted.

The people gathered around a young woman who shouted at a man in his forties. He was holding his injured left shoulder with his right hand. "You keep away from me!" Her eyes bulged; the red lines made them seem like coals of fire.

Both cops reached to restrain the man and young woman to prevent any further fighting.

At precisely that moment, two big men in T-shirts and blue jeans dashed out of the doorway of the row home. Without warning, they attacked VP and CC, who had no time to react.

A man nearby shouted, "Grab his gun and kill him!" At that same moment, however, seven or eight other cops arrived on the scene and battled their way through a growing crowd.

The young woman and man were arrested. VP and CC were taken to a nearby hospital with minor injuries.

While waiting for an evaluation by a doctor, CC was wondering if all of this was worth it. *Why did I choose to become a cop? Should I remain on the force? What is the meaning of life anyway?* His reflections turned to drowsiness, and he drifted off to sleep.

It was a restless stay in the hospital. His sleep was interrupted by the activity in the hallway. He was also suffering from recurring pain and a series of disturbing nightmares. One of those nightmares had a profound impact on his life.

He dreamed about the traumatic experience of that night. He dreamed that one of the men had taken his revolver and shot him three times. He felt the impact of the bullets slugging into his chest, his neck, his forehead. He dreamed the fear, the pain, and the nausea. He dreamed he died.

He went through that long tunnel from this life to the next. But there was no warm radiance, no lights of glory waiting for him; it was pitch darkness, and in the distance, he could see a holocaust. He was transported nearer to it, and as he approached, he could smell the rottenness of putrefying meat, the stench of burnt flesh, and the sulfuric fumes that filled his nostrils with the odor of thousands of spoiled eggs. He could hear torment. People wailed in agony. Shrieks and curses pierced the awful blackness.

> The Son of man shall send forth his angels, and
> they shall gather out of his kingdom all things that
> offend, and them which do iniquity; And shall cast

them into a furnace of fire: there shall be wailing
and gnashing of teeth. (Matthew 13:41, 42)

Soon he entered thick burning smog that was filled with flaming
hot ashes. He felt as if he was in a fiery furnace. His hair was on fire.
He screamed and flailed, but it was useless. Suddenly, he was hurled
into a gigantic pit. He was falling through intensely hot, licking
flames. He knew he was falling, and he began to scream, "No! No!
Water—someone give me water! Help me! God, help me!"

And he cried and said, Father Abraham, have mercy
on me, and send Lazarus, that he may dip the tip
of his finger in water, and cool my tongue; for I am
tormented in this flame. (Luke 16:24)

A nurse had turned on the lights and comforted him, "Officer,
you've only had a bad nightmare. Everything is okay." She fluffed
his pillow, gently rested his head, wiped the perspiration from his
forehead, and gave him a sedative.

The pill did not quite conquer his fear, however, and he stayed
awake for a long time, thinking about the meaning of that terrible
nightmare.

The nightmare was so real. In his mind he had experienced the
torment of great fear.

But the fearful, and unbelieving, and the abominable,
and murderers, and whoremongers, and sorcerers,
and idolaters, and all liars, shall have their part in the
lake which burneth with fire and brimstone: which
is the second death. (Revelation 21:8)

DISPATCH 2

REFLECTIONS

As in water face answereth to face, so the heart of man to man.
—Proverbs 27:19

CC had often heard people say that at a moment close to death their entire lives had flashed before them. His brush with death created in his mind several flashing moments of his past, as if he were reliving his life in supersonic speed.

He thought back to his early days as a child, growing up in a home with an Irish father and Italian mother. He remembered playing stickball on the street with a few of his friends, going to religion classes, and learning to get along with his peers.

He was a daydreamer. Even during the early years of elementary school, he remembered fantasizing about being an air force pilot or even an astronaut. He would sit in class, drawing pictures of jets and imagining he was flying those silver birds through cloudless skies.

His dreaming got him in trouble from time to time, as teachers discovered he wasn't paying attention in class. But there was another problem. He couldn't see the chalkboard.

One very vivid memory resulted from this problem when he was in grade school. That night, while he was lying in his hospital bed reviewing his life, that one experience as a young boy leaped into his mind as a very traumatic and significant event.

One of his teachers, a domineering person who looked much like an army first sergeant, was asking students to read social studies questions that were written on the blackboard and to give the appropriate answers. He couldn't read the questions from his fourth-row seat, but he was embarrassed to sit in front of the class. Nervously, he waited for his turn.

The teacher commanded, "Read question seven!"

He stammered and then attempted to read the question, but the only word he could make out was *what*. It seemed like hours, but it was only a few minutes. His total silence caused all the students to turn and stare at him. His face blushed a bright crimson, and some of the students giggled.

The teacher grimaced, and looking directly at him, shouted, "You never pay attention in class! Unless you straighten up, you will be nothing but a bum!"

Hot tears welled in his eyes. He put his head down in shame as the teacher turned to another classmate.

"Nothing but a bum! Nothing but a bum!" The echo reverberated in his thoughts for several days, and like a foundation with a brick removed, his already poor self-image weakened.

In the darkness of his hospital room, he relived the humiliation and frustration of that day. He realized that this event had strengthened his determination to be somebody—to be a leader, a person other people would admire. Even as a boy, he wanted so much to prove his worth—to the teacher, his classmates, his parents, and himself. He would become somebody.

As he stared at a wall, he asked himself, "But who am I? I was almost killed. People who were wild with hatred and frustration had almost taken my life. Why are people like this? Where is God? What is the meaning of it all?"

His life had always been a search, a thirsting to know, to learn, to achieve. "But what have I accomplished?" he asked.

He remembered his first religious celebration. It was a confusing day for him as an eight-year-old boy. His parents dressed him in a white suit with short pants, and he knew they were joyful and proud. As he went to the altar with his classmates, he looked up at the clergyman, and he imagined he was an angel—or God himself. He could not understand all the excitement, but he enjoyed the day very much, especially the party in his parents' apartment. His grandparents were there, along with many of his aunts and uncles and his cousins. It represented his first truly religious experience, and now he was realizing that he had begun to develop a strong consciousness of God from that moment on.

Soon after this celebration, his parents decided to move from that home to a new home in a new state. When they told CC they would be moving, he felt strong emotions of excitement, sadness, and some fear. He thought it would be an adventure, but he also hated to leave his friends.

Moving to a new neighborhood, school, and city was not easy for him. For a long time, he was afraid to make new friends. His active imagination, however, helped him adjust. He fantasized about his future, by continuing to dream about becoming a pilot or an astronaut.

He remembered how he wanted to be like Superman—a man with special powers who helps others.

By this time his eyesight problem had been diagnosed, and he was fitted with a pair of glasses when he was in sixth grade. He felt very self-conscious when he wore those black-rimmed glasses, so he would only put them on when it was necessary. His schoolwork began to improve, but no one told him that his poor vision would keep him from being an air force pilot.

His reflections of the past had calmed him enough that he eventually drifted off to sleep. Early the next morning the doctor came in and told him he was doing fine and would be returning to work soon.

He asked the doctor how his partner was doing, and the doctor replied that he too was doing fine and expected him to return to work soon.

As the doctor left his room, he closed his eyes briefly and prayed, "God, you spared my life. Thank you. I feel that I don't really know you. Help me to know you better, and to learn what you expect from my life."

> Ask, and it shall be given you; seek, and ye shall find; knock, and it shall be opened unto you. (Matthew 7:7)

When he awakened the next morning, he once again began to reflect on the past, remembering the time when he became cynical, even defiant, and powerless to fight the injustices he saw. He knew he had to find a positive channel to release his negative energy, so he decided to go out for sports—football, baseball, and track. He learned to suppress some of the questioning and searching that seemed to haunt him.

He found a part-time job stocking shelves in a supermarket. There he met a customer named T.

T was an iron worker. He was a big man with a muscular torso who had a reputation of being honest and just. He also had a reputation of being a man of faith. When he spoke to people, he would always talk about the power of prayer. It was T's faith in God more than anything else that left a lifelong impression on everyone who crossed his path, including CC, who looked forward to his long conversations with T.

T had retired from his job and was no longer visiting the supermarket. He was gone. Just like that.

CC rebelled against the church. It wasn't strong enough for him. It didn't have the power to change the world like it was supposed to. It meant nothing to him.

During church services when his parents thought he was

worshiping with the congregation, he would slip out and go to his private place of meditation in the graveyard. To him, the dead were less hypocritical than the living.

He could suppress his search no longer. He had to have answers for the questions that plagued him. He knew he could never be satisfied until he found them.

One Sunday morning CC took a seat on a rotting log beneath a giant oak tree. It was winter, and the sky was gray. A hint of snow was in the air. The trees surrounding the cemetery were bare and lifeless. Everything looked so cold and harsh. He reached down and picked up a tiny pebble. As he tossed it in the air a few times, the realization struck him that life is like the changing seasons. There are stormy times and dark times, but there is sunshine too. His life is like this graveyard—gloomy, meaningless, and cold. It must change, he determined, as he hurled the pebble over a row of tombstones. But that change would not come for many years.

DISPATCH 3

TAKE MY YOKE

Take my yoke upon you and learn of me; for I am meek and
lowly in heart: and ye shall find rest unto your souls.
—Matthew 11:29

Soon after CC graduated high school in 1970, life for him took a
radical turn. "Mister, take that gum out of your mouth!" Red-faced
and angry, Air Force Sergeant W reminded CC of a grizzly raised
on its hind legs and ready to attack. The brim of his hat scraped
CC's forehead as he pushed his face into his. They were nose-to-
nose when this military giant screamed, "I said take that gum out
of your mouth!"

The sergeant pressed the full force of his six-foot-two, 240-pound
frame against him, as he shouted, "You are bothering me!"

The sergeant reminded him that he was now a member of the
US Air Force; and told him he did not have any rights! "We are your
mother, father, sister, and brother!" shouted the sergeant.

With that, Sergeant W took the wad of bubble gum out of CC's
mouth, and with fifty of his fellow recruits watching, stuck it on
CC's nose.

The old resentment burned within the pit of his stomach. It
became a raging fire. All his muscles tightened, his heart began to

pound, and his face flushed red. He could taste the anger—it was so intense.

CC began to tremble and sweat as he clenched his fists. He felt like snarling and growling in the same way a dog does when he is attacked or abused. Rejection and ridicule frequently caused him to lose control.

This time, however, he managed to hold it in. He bit his tongue, gritted his teeth, and swallowed his pride. He really didn't have much choice to do otherwise.

So, this was his welcome into the branch of the service that he had promised to give the next four years of his life.

When CC stepped off the jet on this July morning in the Midwest, he was taken aback by the heat. Unlike what he was used to on the East Coast, where summer evenings turned slightly cooler. It seemed as hot at one thirty in the morning as it would feel during the day. He wondered if he would be able to withstand the heat through all the rigors of basic training.

After graduating from high school, CC had decided to enlist in the air force. His near-sightedness prevented him from becoming a pilot as he had always hoped to be, but by joining the air force, he could also serve his country, and this was important to him.

He had enlisted to become an avionics technician. His job would involve maintenance and repair for C-141 transports, which are Boeing 707s that have been converted into military planes for carrying troops, equipment, and cargo.

Although he enjoyed many aspects of the training he received in boot camp, he felt an almost overwhelming loneliness during the first few months. It was another difficult adjustment.

But there was little opportunity to deal with his feelings. His drill instructors saw to that, with push-ups, sit-ups, pull-ups, bayonet drill, rifle range, marching, infiltration course, hand grenades, and chemical warfare training.

The air force sergeant who greeted him seemed to enjoy staying on his case. It appeared that every time the sergeant met a new band of recruits, he would scan the sea of faces to find individuals he could use as his "whipping boys" throughout the course of basic training. CC concluded that he was Sergeant W's "whipping boy."

Almost invariably, the sergeant would find a punishment for him. He hated cleaning the latrines most of all. Once the sergeant had him dig a four-foot hole just so he (the sergeant) could put his cigarette at the bottom and then have him fill it in again.

CC thrived on the physical labor, however, because it made him feel stronger. In the evenings while sitting in the barracks shining his boots, cleaning his weapon, or writing letters home, he would buy an entire pizza pie from the snack truck that came through the regimental area each night. He would consume the whole pie, along with potatoes he ate. This habit caused him to gain several pounds during his first ten weeks in the service.

His frame filled out, and his muscles grew firmer. He felt healthy, and he learned to be grateful for the assignments he was given.

His pride remained a problem, however. He did not like to be a follower. And he had never responded well to authority. He continued to question everything—especially the decisions of authority figures.

His father had been quite an authoritarian, but he was always fair. The authority he encountered in the air force was different; many times, it was both demanding and unfair. He had to camouflage his arrogant approach to life, but his resentment and defensiveness would not die easily.

One night while lying in bed at the barracks, CC did a lot of thinking while gazing at the heavens. The red blinking lights of aircraft passed over every ten minutes or so, and the bright half-moon seemed to stand watch over the sleeping world. A shooting star raced through the sky and disappeared before it reached the horizon. A glow from the lights of a nearby city filled the lower sky.

The sky in the South seems bigger than it does in most places because there are no mountains and few tall trees. As he looked up at the vast expanse of space he wondered about God. *The universe is so big. Where does it end? Where is heaven? Who is God?* he thought. Eventually he fell asleep, totally exhausted by the old, familiar questions—the questions that have no answers.

Shortly after basic training concluded, CC was assigned to another training base. It was time to enter the next phase—advanced training for military occupational specialties.

As he was getting ready to leave basic training, he ran into Sergeant W at a local store. He had gotten over the humiliation he had experienced that first night and had come to respect this uncompromising man.

As inflexible as Sergeant W was, CC liked him and after a few weeks began to realize that the sergeant was trying to develop certain qualities in him.

During a brief conversation, CC told the sergeant that he helped him change from a boy to a man, as he shook his hand.

Sergeant W replied, "Mister, do you have a piece of gum?"

Soon after arriving at the new training center, CC met another avionics trainee, QM. Both often attended class together, and CC soon realized there was something special about this guy. He always seemed so positive, full of energy, and optimistic. The other guys in the unit frequently ridiculed QM, calling him a "Jesus freak," but he never got angry when they taunted him.

During many conversations, QM would talk about faith, prayer, and Jesus. CC got to a point where he became annoyed and considered QM a "GI Jesus." Someone not to get too close to.

But before they parted ways, QM said something to CC that would stay with him for the rest of his life: "A personal relationship with Jesus Christ will be your gateway to everlasting peace." "Jesus saith unto him, I am the way, the truth, and the life: no man cometh unto the Father, but by me" (John 14:6).

PART 2

THE MAKING OF A COP

DISPATCH 4

CHANGING UNIFORMS

And he answered and spake unto those that stood before him,
saying, Take away the filthy garments from him. And unto him
he said, Behold, I have caused thine iniquity to pass from thee,
and I will clothe thee with change of raiment.
—Zechariah 3:4

After CC was honorably discharged from the air force he began to prepare for his return to civilian life.

Police work held an attraction for him because it enables an individual to serve his city in a very positive and noticeable way. Eventually, he was hired by a police department in New Jersey.

CC met his first partner on the force, a guy named VP, and together they walked the beat through the streets of a very tough city.

CC was twenty-five years old; VP was forty years old—a veteran officer with twenty years of service on the force.

Frequently, as they patrolled the streets, they would encounter young teens who had nothing better to do but hang out and get into trouble.

One night a group of youths were selling newspapers on a dark street corner. One of the teens looked at both cops and told them to get lost. The group of young people who were nearby laughed, and both cops decided to continue their patrol.

CC was a bit aggravated challenging VP as to why he did not arrest the teen who told him to get lost. VP replied, "You have to try to understand where they're coming from. Look at that newspaper."

It was filled with articles and headlines that described the pain and suffering of a lot of people. "What these kids need is Jesus," VP continued as CC gave him a long stare.

VP was dedicated to his work. He demonstrated a genuineness, understanding, and compassion like no other person CC had known. At the same time, he could be tough when he had to be, and the people—especially the kids—respected him and listened to him.

Each time both cops turned into alleys, they would often hear a young voice shout, "Here comes the man!" Kids would shuffle off in all directions. Many of the young people were involved with drugs, gambling, and gang warfare.

VP was dedicated to cleaning up the area. He really wanted to help the young people who lived there. This really impressed CC.

VP's two primary goals were to make the streets safe and to get rid of drugs. Other cops told CC that VP had been given the opportunity to move to a more prestigious position a couple of times, but he had always refused because he felt his work on the streets was incomplete.

When CC began his assignment, it was summer. The heat and humidity combined with the air pollution to make the city a sultry, smelly place of misery. As the boiling July sun beat down on the bricks, sidewalks, and pavements each day until late in the evening, the heat would soak into the concrete, and this made the evenings and nights almost as hot as the daytime. The people were jammed into apartments—third-, fourth-, fifth-, and sixth-floor tenements above stores.

As they patrolled the neighborhoods, they could hear the city— the cries of infants coming from windows overhead—babies who could not sleep because of the hot, unmoving air. Many people leaned out of windows overhead and shouted to their friends. On every street a crowd would gather to discuss the issues and events affecting their lives.

In noisy taverns men and women gathered to forget their misery; the strong, pungent smell of alcohol and stale tobacco smoke would waft through open doorways and hang like a heavy cloud. The blare of jukeboxes throbbed the latest hits. Cars squealed around corners as their rubber tires glided across the hot pavement.

Graffiti on every wall and sign revealed that perhaps VP was right. These young people needed Jesus.

All of this was the city, and it was hard to get used to.

One oppressive night, VP and CC went into a corner grocery store and met an older heavy-set woman who was sitting on a wooden crate behind a candy counter.

VP asked for two Cokes, and she rose slowly, walked over to the refrigerator and took out two bottles. She limped over to the counter where both cops were standing, opened the bottles with a rusty can opener tied to a string, and gave them to CC.

He took a good look at this old lady and thought about what kinds of suffering she had endured throughout her life. Her gray hair was tied in a bun, but loose strands sprung out in all directions. Her forehead was beaded with sweat, and she frequently took a paper towel from her apron to wipe away the moisture. She was bent with age, and her excess weight seemed to tax both her ability to breathe and to walk.

As they began to drink their sodas, she sat back down, leaned over, and asked CC a question. "Officer, could you just answer me one question?"

He nodded. "Sure, Ma'am. Go ahead."

Two young kids who were at the pinball machine stopped playing and turned in their direction.

The old lady wheezed, looked up, and spoke with a tone of

defiance. "Well, if the police are so mighty and so powerful, why can't you stop all the robbing, mugging, and looting?"

CC stammered, then said, "It takes everybody to get the job done. Crime and evil know no barriers—we're all affected."

She hung her head and shrugged, "Yeah, but how did it all begin?" She was expressing an honest frustration. What was the answer? Conflict is everywhere. The young against the old, black against white, Arab against Jew. Although CC decided not to answer her question, he grew even more determined to find some answers. *What can I, as a cop, do to improve race relations? Can I make a lasting contribution?*

As both cops started to leave the store, she looked up at CC and said, "It began with sin. The Bible tells us, "for the wages of sin is death" (Romans 6:23). VP smiled as if to agree with this woman, and a chill ran up and down CC's spine.

After working with VP for a year—a period of apprenticeship— an official from another police department approached CC to see if he would be interested in becoming a cop in his city. The official explained he would first have to complete a year of being a probationary officer, then take a police exam to get the job full time and permanently.

CC was thrilled to be considered for this position. He would be close to home and knew that this new police force had a fine reputation that was known throughout the Northeast.

That night in their patrol car CC told VP about his plan and thanked him for all he taught him. VP encouraged him and told him he was on his way to a successful career.

It is funny how close two cops can get when they patrol the streets together night after night. You learn a lot about each other— the other's strengths and weaknesses as well as your own. Cops often say that they spend more time with their partners than with their spouses, and so, as in a marriage, very few facades can remain. Two cops working together can really get to know each other. CC knew he would miss VP because he had become like a real brother to him.

CC and VP had been through several close calls together, including the confrontation described in an earlier chapter of this book.

But VP understood, and during his last conversation with CC he told him, "that woman in the store was right. It began with sin, and the wages of sin is death."

Then with a twinkle in his eye and smile on his face, VP concluded, "But the gift of God is eternal life, through Jesus Christ our Lord" (Romans 6:23).

DISPATCH 5

A NEW COMMANDER

Behold, I have given him for a witness to the people,
a leader and commander to the people.
—Isaiah 55:4

It was July 4, 1977, and CC had begun his work as a probationary patrolman at his new police department. At nine on this Independence Day morning he was awakened by his telephone. Usually no one called him so early—especially on his day off.

When he answered the phone, it was the mayor calling to tell him to be in his office at 10:00 a.m., sharp!

At first, he thought someone might be playing a joke on him. But no, it really was the mayor. "Why does he want to see me? Did I do something wrong? It had to be important for him to call me on a holiday." Quickly preparing, he put on his uniform and took off for the mayor's office.

The mayor was a rock of a man who stood over six feet tall, dressed impeccably, and projected an air of contentment and charisma.

CC knocked on the door of the mayor's office. To his surprise, the mayor himself opened the door. After inviting him in, he told him to sit down to wait for another officer. He went back to his desk and began doing some paperwork.

After waiting approximately twenty minutes, the other officer arrived, and the mayor opened the door. An officer who CC had seen before walked in.

The mayor said, "This is your new partner, OC."

As CC and OC shook hands, the mayor told them to sit down.

"I called both of you here today to discuss a confidential matter that I wish to go no further than this office," said the mayor. Both cops sat up in their chairs and leaned forward.

"We have a very serious problem developing, and something must be done at once to reckon with it. Our parks and other areas of the city are running rampant with teenagers who are drinking alcohol, taking drugs, and vandalizing private property. Some people even fear for their lives; they want to see something done that will correct this problem."

"What would you like us to do, sir?" OC asked.

"Well, after reviewing your performance records as patrolmen, I have concluded that you are the best two qualified throughout the entire police force to handle this problem. Consequently, you both will be taken off your shifts on Monday, and your new hours will be from 7:00 p.m. to 3:00 a.m. You will dress in plain clothes, and you will be under the command of the deputy chief."

"Yes, sir," both responded. Feeling slightly overwhelmed, CC said, "We'll get the job done, your honor."

Perhaps sensing their anxiety, the mayor said, "Now I don't expect miracles, but I have confidence that you both can do this important job."

"Thank you. We'll do our best," OC assured him.

Both cops shook hands with the mayor, and as they were leaving the building, CC suggested that they go for a cup of coffee. Having a cup of coffee together began a long and significant relationship that was to last many years.

While sipping the hot java, the cops learned all they could about each other. OC had been working as a patrolman for several years. CC had only a couple years' experience.

OC was thirty-eight; CC was a decade younger. Even though there were great differences between them, they really seemed to hit it off that morning. Where CC was aggressive and impulsive and eager to get the job done, OC was more patient—always thinking things through. He was more cautious; CC would take risks. CC was quick-tempered; OC could more easily roll with the punches. Both cops agreed that it would work out because their differences would provide a good balance. They could become an effective team. The mayor had made a good decision.

My social life will certainly have to change now, CC realized as he headed for his apartment. He was living away from home, by himself, but his life had taken on a bit of a wild image. Nonetheless, he still felt challenged and thrilled by the possibilities connected with this new assignment.

Why did the mayor pick us for this assignment? How will we be able to approach the problem? What will it be like to work with OC?

Monday finally arrived, and CC had not seen or spoken with OC until six forty-five that evening when they both reported to police headquarters to start their new assignment. The desk sergeant directed them to the deputy chief's office.

Both cops hardly spoke as they walked down the corridor. Approaching the deputy chief's office, they looked at each other nervously. CC was dressed in blue jeans and a short-sleeved shirt, and OC was wearing a leisure suit and a bright yellow shirt. OC knocked on the door of the deputy chief's office. There was no answer. He tried the knob, but the door was locked.

CC asked, "What do we do now?"

They walked to the detective bureau offices, and a clerk told them that the deputy chief had gone home for the day. Puzzled, the cops briefly discussed what their next step would be.

"Let's go to another superior officer and see what he recommends," CC suggested.

"Good idea," OC concurred.

They soon discovered that no one knew about their assignment—it was totally confidential. They called the deputy chief at his home.

The deputy chief told them to begin an investigation on a matter he left at the front desk for both to look at. He said that he would call the desk sergeant and have him assign a car to them.

CC realized then that they would be much on their own in figuring out how to tackle problems—and in developing solutions. He liked the feeling of autonomy this gave to him, and he realized then how much confidence the mayor had placed in him and OC.

He turned to OC. "Let's go get our car, partner."

"Great," he answered as they walked back to the desk sergeant.

They were given an unmarked police vehicle—a maroon 1974 Fury. It looked like it was one hundred years old. Both cops just stood there and looked at it. "I wonder if it runs?" CC laughed.

He opened the door and looked at the odometer. "Only 87,000 miles, but it's ours," he remarked.

It had a couple of dents in the right rear fender and the front grill work had been replaced by a heavy-duty metal screen. Although their policeman's pride in a good appearance was a bit disturbed, they knew that such a vehicle could make their work even more effective because no one would ever guess that cops were driving such a car!

They got in for their test run. During the first hour on the road, they got to know each other—and the car—very well. To start the car, for example, you could not use the accelerator because it would flood the engine.

They drove to one of the city parks. This place was a favorite hangout for teenagers at night. They got out of the car and began to stroll casually down one of the lanes that go alongside a brook.

"What kind of work did you do at your old police department?" OC asked.

"I patrolled inner-city streets with my partner. There was a lot of crime there."

"I'll bet you learned a lot about human nature. How did you feel about your work there?" OC inquired.

"Well, frankly, it upset me a good part of the time. There was so much misery. People seemed bent on destroying themselves and one another. I really felt bad for the young people especially. It almost seems like the world is falling apart."

The cops sat down on a park bench to continue their discussion. It was approaching twilight, and many of the activities in the park were beginning to die down. Little boys packed up their fishing gear and headed home. Young mothers pushing strollers and carriages walked by them on their way back to their cars. The bike riders, both young and old, began to disappear. They were replaced by middle-aged men, now home from work, who used the path for jogging. A strange quietness hovered over the park.

CC told OC, "The phoniness of people is disgusting. I don't think there's any hope for anyone to live a decent life on this planet." Even as he said these words, CC realized that this guy had gotten to the real him. CC was opening in a way that he had seldom done before. "What's with this guy?" he wondered. "Why is he asking me these questions? Why am I confiding in him?"

OC said, "You seem angry. Why do you feel this way?"

"I've seen too much phoniness and suffering. I could go on and on telling you about all the violence—the destruction I've seen."

OC placed his hand on his partner's shoulder sympathizing with him.

"It's just that sometimes I wonder what the purpose of it all is. Where is there any meaning in this life?" CC continued.

"CC, there's hope in Jesus Christ. He alone can give a person purpose. You need to give your life to Him," OC replied.

The impact of his statement hit CC with the force of a

thunderbolt. It shattered his defenses like a cannonball crashing through a wall. It reached his heart. The raw honesty of the moment both hurt and felt good. He was troubled and yet at peace. He was confused and yet he could think clearly. It was as if a new mind—a new approach to life—was taking over.

"I do believe in God, OC, and I guess one day He will straighten it all out."

But OC was not about to let his partner pass off the matter so lightly because he could see the raging storm of conflict within him. He went on to press for a decision—a commitment. He asked CC a question that no one had ever asked before: "If you were to die right now, would you go to heaven?"

The question was so blatant that it shocked him. "Well, I don't know for sure, but I think God would probably send me to heaven because I've tried to lead a decent life. I've never hurt anyone."

"Did you ever read the Bible?" OC asked.

"Only a few times. There was this airman in the service who gave me a New Testament to read, and I guess I looked at it a few times. The same guy had told me that I should become a born-again Christian."

> Jesus answered and said unto him, Verily, verily, I say unto thee, except a man be born again, he cannot see the kingdom of God. (John 3:3)

"And how did you answer him?"

"I told him I had better things to do—that he could worship God his way, and I would worship my way."

"And have you been worshipping God?"

CC felt that his partner was getting too close for comfort and started getting fidgety and uncomfortable.

"No, I must admit that I hardly ever go to church anymore. I feel like there's this big, empty void within me. I do want to know God better."

— 25 —

"Jesus Christ can fill that void," OC assured CC as he handed him a New Testament and showed him the Gospel of John. "Read chapter 3, and ask God to help you to understand it," he directed.

"I will. I'll read it when I get home."

The cops got up from the bench and continued their survey of the park and the discussion of their new assignment. They did not talk about God anymore that evening until they got back to headquarters.

"Hey, OC, by the way, what religion are you?" (The subject had been on his mind all evening.)

"I'm a born-again Christian," he answered.

"Thanks for talking with me tonight."

"You're welcome; don't forget to read John chapter 3."

"Okay," he answered.

"Good night, friend. See you tomorrow."

No other cars were on the street as CC drove home around 3:00 a.m. His mind was racing with thoughts, and he knew he would not be able to sleep for a while. He drove around for several minutes.

The moon was full, and there wasn't a cloud in the sky. He drove past a small chapel that was on the edge of a cemetery on the outskirts of the city. He stopped and got out of the car.

The chapel was a white-frame building, distinguished only by its steeple with a simple cross on top. The light of the moon gave everything a glowing quality—the little church, the gravestones behind it, and the cross. The wind began to blow through nearby pine trees, and he felt an eerie chill run up his spine.

The cemetery reminded him of the place where he had spent many hours thinking and meditating as a boy—behind his family's church. He remembered all the questions and how he had challenged Jesus to give him the answers. The resentment he had felt toward the church—and God—came floating to the surface once more, and he began to feel sorry—even guilty—for those feelings and his attitude in general.

Suddenly the sky above the chapel brightened. The chill was replaced by a feeling of warmth that surged upward from the pit of his stomach to flood his entire being like a fountain would fill a pool. He was in a sort of trance. Tears came to his eyes, as he stared at a concrete crucifix with Jesus hanging on the cross looking directly at him.

He remembered reading about a Roman soldier thrusting a spear in the side of the Savior. "But one of the soldiers with a spear pierced his side, and forthwith came there out blood and water" (John 19:34).

Yet, Jesus did not even grimace. CC envisioned Jesus as a person with such empathy, such understanding, such love. And then it hit him! Jesus had died for him. The revelation exploded within the heart and soul of CC, and he began to feel ashamed as his thoughts disappeared.

"All the times I had rejected Him, doubted Him and turned against Him. And yet He loved me—He died for me," thought CC. Unlike the cold, stone crucifix in the cemetery, he had felt in his heart a living Jesus, and he knew He loved him.

CC felt such a deep certainty of His acceptance, and he was sure that Christ was directing his life. He felt so clean, so renewed, and the peace He had imparted was so wonderful.

CC felt the presence of Christ, and He knew He could never be the same. Yes, his new commander for life would be Jesus Christ!

DISPATCH 6

SUCCESS

This Book of the Law shall not depart out of thy mouth,
but thou shalt meditate therein day and night, that thou
mayest observe to do according to all that is written
therein. For then thou shalt make thy way prosperous,
and then thou shalt have good success.
—Joshua 1:8

CC could hardly wait to see OC and tell him what had happened
to him. Before leaving for work he opened the New Testament that
OC gave him and turned to chapter 3 of the Gospel of John. As he
began to read, the wonderful peace and joy he had felt that morning
returned and filled his being.

"Except a man be born again, he cannot see the kingdom of
God" (John 3:3). "What did Jesus mean?" he wondered. "This must
be where the phrase, born-again Christian comes from."

As he read on, he began to realize that Jesus wants each one of
us to give our lives over to Him—to start a new life with Him at the
controls instead of going along in our stubborn, independent way.

"Jesus, I want to be born again," CC prayed. "Please show me
how to be born again. Come into my life. Change me."

At six thirty he met OC at police headquarters. They got into
their unmarked car, and immediately he began to tell him what had

transpired that morning. They drove to the top of a secluded hill that overlooked the city and stopped. CC could tell that his partner was happy for him.

"CC, do you sincerely feel in your heart that you want to have a personal relationship with Jesus Christ?" OC asked.

"I sure do. To think that Jesus died on the cross for me so that I could live is mind-boggling. I think it's about time I did things His way."

OC's eyes reflected a deep sense of joy. "Then let's join in a simple prayer. Lord God, I confess that I am a sinner. At times I have made a mess of things. I admit that I can't do this alone anymore. I am coming to you, letting you know from my heart that I truly believe Jesus came to this earth, shed his blood, and rose from the dead so that every sin I have ever committed may be forgiven. I believe that Jesus sits at the right hand of the Father and that one day we will meet. I now accept Jesus Christ as my personal Lord, Savior, and Master. Amen."

> For God so loved the world, that he gave his only begotten Son, that whosoever believeth in him should not perish, but have everlasting life. (John 3:16)

In tears, both men clenched their hands together as if to seal the commitment, and CC proclaimed, "I know I'm a born-again Christian now too!"

"Yes," OC responded, "you are, and your life will never be the same."

It seemed as if all CC's questions had disappeared. It was because he had found the answer. He now had a purpose for life.

They were two born-again cops. They had a third partner too—the Lord Jesus Christ. Every night as they patrolled the streets, both cops would share the good news of Jesus with each other.

For where two or three are gathered together in my name, there am I in the midst of them. (Matthew 18:20)

Numerous complaints were coming into police headquarters from residents who lived near a dense wooded area. They reported that mobs of young people would gather in the woods each evening to drink, take drugs, and go on a rampage, destroying property and terrorizing the neighborhood. Both cops decided to make this situation their number-one priority.

They gave surveillance to the wooded area in question. It was a very dark and dense area that was situated on a hill that sloped down into the back yards of homes on either side. The houses were typical of the upper-middle-class city. Many were bilevels with well-groomed yards, two-car garages, and swimming pools.

During daytime hours, the area was a quiet neighborhood where people could live peaceably, enjoying their gardens, pools, and patios. After nightfall, however, it became an entirely different place—a place of fear, sleepless nights, and worry.

Fences had been broken down, above-ground swimming pools had been damaged, windows had been broken, and walls of homes had been defaced with paint. Some cars had been broken into, and all the neighbors were growing tense and anxious.

That night OC and his partner walked into the woods at dusk and stationed themselves in a secluded area remarkably close to one of the spots where young people would gather. What they saw sickened them. Groups of kids were meeting in the dark of night, then tramping through the neighborhood, shouting, screaming, and laughing. They broke bottles and threw eggs at homes, and someone smashed a rock through a picture window.

Both cops soon realized they were not dealing with a few kids "having fun," but were dealing with a large group of young people—some of whom were drug addicts whose minds were out of control.

They gathered as much information as they could and soon

discovered that Friday nights were the big party nights for these kids. They also had succeeded in finding out who was supplying the liquor and who was selling the drugs—both pot and LSD.

After about two weeks of surveillance, OC and CC decided to develop a plan of attack. They reported to the detective bureau and filed their confidential reports that revealed the information they had obtained.

They then prayed, "Lord, please give us wisdom in dealing with this situation." "If any of you lack wisdom, let him ask of God, that giveth to all men liberally, and upbraideth not; and it shall be given him" (James 1:5).

They requested a minimum of five men to assist them in a raid on the next Friday night party. They were outnumbered by at least ten to one because frequently dozens of young people would gather for these parties. They felt it could be "suicide" for just the two of them to attempt the raid by themselves. They walked home that night and talked about the importance of keeping this matter in prayer.

The next evening, they learned that the police department had attempted to raid these groups before. But every time the police had approached the gathering, the young people had scattered, successfully escaping the police altogether. The police suspected that the kids had lookouts posted to alert them of their arrival. But where would they go? No one seemed to have any idea.

CC and OC also learned that they would not be permitted to have any extra men on this assignment. They would have to tackle it alone.

They went to the precise location where the kids partied the night before. They examined the entire area to look for clues that might lead them to where they were running to—their secret hiding place.

Literally hundreds of broken beer bottles littered the entire wooded area. Not a single clue turned up.

"Now what?" asked CC. "It certainly doesn't look very good," replied OC.

They began to feel sorry for themselves. It seemed as if all their planning and searching had been to no avail.

They began walking back to the location of the previous evening's party, taking a second look at the area.

"Hey, OC, come over here!" CC shouted as he tramped through a wooded section. OC quickly ran through the brush to see what he had found.

"Look, here's a camouflaged path. We must have stumbled over it several times. See how they've covered it with leaves and brush to prevent anyone from detecting their footprints?"

They scraped back some of the leaves and brush and uncovered a well-worn path that was filled with footprints.

"Good work. Let's see where this leads," OC said.

As they followed the path, they noticed that the entire perimeter had been carefully hidden. Trees and bushes had been uprooted from other areas of the park and replanted in a circular area that completely covered the entrance to a hideout. Unless you had known of its existence, it would have been virtually impossible to find.

As they found their way through the bushes and shrubbery, they came to a hollow area under a group of trees. There was a hideout-like crevasse carved into one small hillside, and as they entered it, they noticed a space that looked like a one-room apartment. It was furnished with a couple of old armchairs, a double-bed mattress, and pillows and blankets that had been carefully placed on the ground. There was even a large woven rug covering the ground.

Using their flashlights, they examined the entire space. They found a cache of pills, beer bottles, bottles of rum, vodka, and whiskey, and a few nearly empty plastic bags containing traces of marijuana.

"This is it. They never really ran back to their homes or other locations. They have a clubhouse right here."

"Yeah. Instead of leaving the park as the police had suspected, they hid right under their noses. No wonder they were unable to find them previously."

The cops returned to police headquarters, and while they were sitting in their office, they bowed their heads and gave God thanks for His answer to their prayers.

DISPATCH 7

FAITH

But without faith it is impossible to please him: for he
that cometh to God must believe that he is, and that
he is a rewarder of them that diligently seek him.
—Hebrews 11:6

Before the Lord came into CC's life, he always found himself trying
to conform to the stereotype of cops that he had seen on TV; this
put a strain on him because it caused him to pretend to be something
different from who he really was.

CC was very ambitious. He wanted to make a lot of arrests so he
could impress the mayor, the chief of police, his fellow cops—and
himself. He had put on a very callous front and tried to come across
like a tough guy.

Soon after he learned about Jesus, however, he experienced a
wonderful sense of inner peace. The striving seemed to settle down
some; he was much more himself. Now he could be used by God,
to help Him show people—both civilians and his fellow cops—that
there is something—someone—to live for. What a difference this
made to his whole perspective on life.

OC and CC would often study the scriptures. One evening OC
pointed out a passage he had never seen before.

"CC, did you know that the Bible talks about cops?"

"No, does it really? Show me where."

OC opened his Bible to the New Testament and said, "I am reading from Romans 13: 'For he is the minister of God to thee for good. But if thou do that which is evil, be afraid; for he beareth not the sword in vain. for he is the minister of God, a revenger to execute wrath upon him that doeth evil' (Romans 13:4). This verse refers to government officials—and I would venture to say that includes cops (those who bear 'not the sword in vain'). We're ministers of God, my brother!"

CC's probationary period as a police officer in this city was now ending. Soon he would have to take a competitive exam in order to get a full-time position with his new police force. He applied for the exam, and although the prospect of this test had scared him during this probationary term, he felt peaceful and confident about his performance.

In his zeal, CC was telling everyone that God would answer his prayers and help him pass the test. He didn't fully realize it at the time, but his constant speaking about God turned some of the other guys off. Many of them left discouraging notes on his locker or made wisecracks about how he would flunk the test.

As he learned more about the exam, some of the old fears began to return. He would be competing against thousands of people from all over the state. The police department he was working at had only one opening.

CC prayed night and day that he would pass the exam. He received strength and faith by reading many scriptures, such as: "For promotion cometh neither from the east, nor from the west, nor from the south. But God is the judge. he putteth down one, and setteth up another" (Psalm 75:6–7).

A fellow officer, who despised CC's Christian commitment, challenged him one day, saying, "Hey, you'd better come off your high horse and stop all your dreaming! There's no way you could be number one—out of thousands of candidates. You're a bigger fool than I thought you were!"

His words cut CC to the quick. For a moment he felt as if he might react like he had before becoming a Christian. But he remembered the Word of God: "Be still, and know that I am God: I will be exalted among the heathen, I will be exalted in the earth" (Psalm 46:10).

Immediately, the tension ceased, and CC simply walked away as the other officer said to him, "There is no God. You are just tricking yourself. You'll see when the exam is over."

Other men on the force began to rib CC a lot as well.

"I had a friend who had his degree in police science and criminology, and he still failed the test."

"You don't know how difficult the questions are, hot dog."

"You'll sweat; you'll squirm; you'll loosen your collar, and you'll come out of the exam looking like a whipped puppy."

After a while, these remarks began to take their toll on his emotions. He was scared and felt rejected. His confidence was ebbing away. It was a dark time, but one night, only a couple of days before he would have to take the exam, as he was lying in his bed praying, he opened his Bible and read, "Trust in the Lord with all thine heart; and lean not unto thine own understanding" (Proverbs 3:5).

Early on a Saturday morning CC got in his car for the hour-and-a-half drive to the exam center. He wanted to trust the Lord, but he kept feeling anxiety attacks all the way there.

When the monitor presented the exam papers to him, he immediately thought about a scripture verse he read a few days ago: "Be careful for nothing; but in everything by prayer and supplication with thanksgiving let your requests be made known unto God. And the peace of God, which passeth all understanding, shall keep your hearts and minds through Christ Jesus" (Philippians 4:6–7).

He started to feel calm and began to answer the questions with a facility and speed that startled him. He could not believe how easy the test seemed to be.

Before most of the others had completed their work, CC was finished. He stood up to turn in his papers, and he gazed around at the hundreds of heads throughout the vast auditorium. A surge of confidence gushed through him as he walked to the front. He believed he passed the test and would get the job. He would not receive the results of the exam for several weeks.

DISPATCH 8

"BLUE" ANGELS

For there stood by me this night the angel of God,
whose I am, and whom I serve, Saying, Fear not.
—Acts 27:23–24

On Friday of the week following the exam, OC and his partner, CC,
planned to raid the teenagers' hangout. All day long they mapped
out their strategy. They would have no help in executing their plans.

It was an unusually quiet and very balmy night. At ten they
parked their car three blocks from the site where they would enter
the wooded area. They were dressed in jeans, sport shirts, and
carried empty beer bottles to make it appear that they were part of
the crowd. As they made their way up a hill, they could hear the
noise of kids walking in the woods. Both cops climbed up a small
embankment and stood about seventy-five yards from where they
had gathered.

Even from a distance they could detect the sweet smell of
marijuana. Suddenly, as if on cue, the crowd erupted, their shouts
and cries intensified, and before the cops knew what happened, the
still night's silence turned into a terror-filled bedlam.

Through their binoculars the cops could see that there were
dozens of young people gathered. Shrieks and screams pierced the
muggy night. A loud crack cut through the low-hanging air—it

was the sound of a bang, and immediately both cops wondered if it was a shot.

As they began to run toward the noise, they heard sounds of bottles smashing, shouting, and then additional bangs from large fireworks thundered into the darkness. The air was filled with the static electricity of terror and rage.

As the cops approached the group, they jumped over a brook and hid in some nearby bushes.

"This is worse than I thought," OC admitted.

"Yeah," CC answered. "There are at least a dozen kids out there, and I can see that a lot of them are high."

The cops had been able to learn that a guy named Z was likely to be their suspect as the supplier of drugs and alcohol. They could see that he was there, and he appeared to be the ringleader. A major part of their plan was to apprehend Z first, if possible, because they felt that the other young people would discontinue their illegal activities if he was out of the picture. But still, there were a lot of them and only two cops.

"These kids are in a reckless state of mind," CC whispered.

"They're almost out of control now," OC observed as the crescendo of screams intensified. They were like a group of rioting prisoners.

"Let's pray for God's wisdom and protection before we proceed. We cannot abandon our efforts now; we're too close," said OC.

Both cops sat still for a moment, prayed, and waited for the right time to move on the crowd. It was now ten thirty, and they were prepared to remain in those bushes until sunrise if necessary.

Silently, they waited and listened. Amid the raucous revelry that was taking place only a few feet from them, they heard another loud sound like a shot. A girl began to scream.

What's wrong with these kids? CC thought as they continued to wait for the right time to move in.

Most of these young people were from upper-middle-class

families, and yet they were giving themselves over to bizarre beliefs. It all seemed so pointless.

The mosquitoes buzzed around the cops and enjoyed a good meal as they repeatedly bit them while they continued to watch, listen, and wait. The night grew darker. It was now midnight.

The gang of young people had grown more subdued. Most of them were sitting down now in little clusters of three or four people and talking more quietly. It was a hot, humid night. One of the boys stood up and lit a cigarette.

In a few moments OC reached into his pocket and once again took out his small Bible and turned to a scripture verse and read it to his partner: "The night is far spent. The day is at hand, let us therefore cast off the works of darkness, and let us put on the armour of light" (Romans 13:12).

OC said, "That is a verse from Romans 13, the chapter we discussed about cops. It is through His Word that we gain strength and faith."

Like a forest fire that dies down and is rekindled by the wind, the violence of the mob rose once more and erupted into a full-flamed conflagration of noise and rioting. Beer and wine bottles smashed against the trees; two boys began to fight, and a boiling rage fed the flames of violence as if gasoline had been thrown on a blazing inferno.

It was time for the cops to make their move. It was 1:00 a.m., and things were really getting out of hand. They were certain that the drugs and alcohol these young people had consumed unleashed their bizarre behavior.

OC and CC got up and began to walk toward the group. They kept their eyes on Z.

OC and his partner held onto their empty beer bottles and pretended to be drunk as they staggered toward the group.

As the cops approached the young people, they were startled by a young man who jumped up out of a row of bushes.

He demanded, "Give me one of those bottles, man." Staggering toward them, he grabbed a bottle. "This is empty," he slurred as he hurled the bottle toward one of the nearby houses.

The sound of shattering glass told OC and CC that he had broken the windshield of a car parked below. This man was drunk, his face was unshaved, and his clothes looked like he had been wearing them for at least a month. The odor of alcohol on his breath broadcasted his condition for several feet around him. He seemed to be yelling at his own mother as he turned toward the home where the car had been parked.

Both cops continued toward the group. "Z is in for a surprise tonight," CC said to OC as they continued their walk.

"He sure is," OC replied.

"Yeah, some of the kids have told the cops how he likes to brag about being so powerful and how he has successfully evaded the police so far, but tonight he is going to meet his match."

Within ten feet of the group a girl spotted OC and CC and shouted, "The cops! Get out of here, everybody!" The group quickly dispersed, scattering in all directions.

OC and CC decided to go after the girl first because she was so much closer than the others. They ran down an embankment, through a row of back yards, and out into the street, where they arrested her. They then called for a marked car to come and pick her up and returned to the woods.

When they arrested the girl, they realized that she was only about fifteen years old. She had sobbed and pleaded with them not to arrest her. It was a bit shocking to understand that they were dealing with children—confused children who were simply looking for love and understanding and could find that kind of acceptance only in their peer group and their irresponsible leader.

They are victims in a very real sense, OC thought as they headed for the hideout where others were huddled.

"Let's go after Z next." OC urged. "We know where he is; that's for sure. Now we have to decide how we will flush him out of that hideout."

CC wondered how many were at the hideout.

"They'll probably feel like trapped animals in there and attack us if we go in."

They got within fifteen feet of the entrance to the hideout. They could see the trees above them silhouetted against the faintly lighted night sky.

OC and his partner crouched in a nearby sewer culvert to make more observations before they moved in.

"The kids think they're safe," OC observed. "They have no idea that we know the existence of this hiding place."

"Yeah, we have the element of surprise on our side," CC replied.

OC said, "There is a verse in the book of Psalms, and it keeps coming to my mind: "For he shall give his angels charge over thee, to keep thee in all thy ways" (Psalm 91:11).

Both cops began to creep cautiously toward the entrance to the hideout. A chilling fear rushed down their spines. It seemed as if the area grew darker and darker. The air became cold and clammy.

CC became chilled and broke out in a cold sweat. The fear was back.

OC said, "Stop. Let's pray before we make another move."

> Ye are of God, little children, and have overcome
> them: because greater is he that is in you, than he
> that is in the world. (1 John 4:4)

Standing straight and tall, both cops marched into the hideout's entrance.

"Freeze!" they shouted, and not a person in the hideout moved.

No one uttered a word. OC walked over to Z and asked him to give him what he held in his hands. It was a bag of pills.

The cops read them their rights and arrested twelve young people for violating the narcotic laws.

One by one, they were marched out of the hideout, and CC radioed police headquarters for a van that would take them all to the station.

OC turned to Z and asked, "Why didn't any of you try to attack us when we entered the hideout?"

"You think I'm crazy or something? There were at least twenty of you guys, and it would have been stupid to think about attacking or running," he answered.

"Twenty? No, Z, there were only two of us and twelve of you."

"Wait a minute," he said, scratching his head and turning to a young girl next to him and asking, "How many cops came into the hideout?"

"Oh, I don't know for sure," she responded. "But there were an awful lot of them."

At that moment, OC and CC looked at each other and thought, *Could it be?* as both remembered reading Psalm 91:11 earlier in the evening.

The weeks went by rather quickly. Only about one month remained before CC's probationary period as a patrolman would be over. He was still waiting to learn the results of the exam.

DISPATCH 9

PROMOTION

Promotion cometh neither from the east, nor from
the west, nor from the south. But God is the judge,
He putteth down one, and setteth up another.
—Psalm 75:6–7

The scores were finally released. CC had told everyone that he would
finish first place out of thousands of candidates, and he believed
this would be true. The marks were posted on the bulletin board at
headquarters.

He could not believe his eyes. He had finished in forty-fourth
place! Totally humiliated and crushed, he ran down to the locker
room, sat on a bench, and began to question his faith. The feeling
of devastation was bad.

His pride and ego were still a big problem. Here he had bragged
to all his family and fellow cops about how he would finish in first
place, and he ended up being number forty-four. The disappointment
was overwhelming.

A couple of the guys who had been ribbing him all along came
down and started their chorus once again. "What happened to the
God you were talking about?" "Number forty-four is a long way
from number one!"

At home that night he got on his knees and said, "Jesus, I read in the Bible, "Let your conversation be without covetousness; and be content with such things as ye have: for he hath said, I will never leave thee, nor forsake thee" (Hebrews 13:5).

"What did I do wrong? Please show me," CC prayed to God.

The next day he went to work and found a big sign on his locker. "Countdown—thirty-five days! You're fired, number one!"

One sergeant took him aside almost like a father would and said that he felt sorry for him and wished him the best.

That evening CC went home and went to sleep. The next day after he awakened, he opened a newspaper while eating breakfast at his kitchen table. On the front page he spotted an article that interested him immediately. It reported that the state legislature passed a residency bill that gave residents of certain cities first preference in police jobs.

CC thought, "Wow!" The candidates on the list he was on revealed that numbers one through forty-three lived outside the city he was seeking to become a police officer in! This meant that he was elevated to number one after all!"

The attitudes of his fellow cops began to change. One of the men who had ridiculed him the most came to him the next day and said, "I don't know how you did it, but you did it. Congratulations."

As he shook the officer's hand, CC remembered the Bible verse he read a few weeks earlier: "For promotion cometh neither from the east, nor from the west, nor from the south. But God is the judge he putteth down one, and setteth up another" (Psalm 75:6–7). The rest is history!

Several months after passing the exam, OC and CC were summoned to the mayor's office. For a while, they wondered if they were being called on the carpet for some oversight.

As they entered his office, they noticed that the chief of police was there also. Their hearts jumped into their throats because they felt even more certain that they were in for a reprimand.

The mayor gestured. "Come in, boys. I'm sure you both know the chief, so I'll dispense with any formal introduction."

They sat down, and the mayor began to tell them how proud he and the chief were regarding the favorable responses they had received concerning them from the public.

The chief turned toward them and said, "You know, when we first put you on this special duty assignment, we had no idea that you would accomplish as much as you did. We are very proud of you, and we want to reward you for your meritorious service to the police force and the city."

The mayor then stood up, picked up two envelopes from the top of his desk, and handed them to both cops. He said, "Open them."

They looked at each other, wondering what the contents of the envelope would say. It was one of the greatest thrills of their lives when they read: "Because of your meritorious service to the police department and the city, you have been promoted to the rank of detective."

It was signed by the chief of police. It is difficult to describe how encouraged and gratified they felt by this. To become a detective is something every cop dreams of attaining. OC and CC had hoped this would happen, but they thought it was years down the road.

They were speechless. The chief got up and asked them to stand while he pinned their new gold badges on them. He said, "You have earned this promotion. We know that your work as detectives will be exemplary. Congratulations, men."

They shook hands with the chief and the mayor, thanked them and then left the office.

In the hallway, OC turned to CC and said, "You know what we have to do, don't you?" CC nodded his head in agreement and told him that he would pick him up at seven that evening.

That night they went to the top of the hill where they had prayed together many times, and they looked up toward the stars sparkling throughout the heavens and lifted their new badges toward the sky and praised and thanked the Lord for His goodness.

> But thou art holy, O thou that inhabitest the praises of Israel. (Psalm 22:3)

DISPATCH 10

THEY THREW US A BONE

As with a sword in my bones, mine enemies reproach
me, while they say daily unto me, where is thy God?
—Psalm 42:10

On November 21, 1980, the detectives reported to the detective
bureau. They had already been together a few years and discovered
that their new roles did not permit them to work together as often
as they had in the past.

In late December, however, they were given an assignment that
required them to work together. One officer remarked, "Several
other men have worked on this particular case for many months,
and they have come up with no clues, so someone has decided to
throw you a bone."

"That doesn't sound too good," OC responded. "But if a bone
is all we've got, we'll have to work with it."

Another detective, who had years of experience on the force,
smirked as if to say, "You guys don't know what's up. You'll never
crack this case."

They knew that they had no choice but to solve this case. If
they blew it, they might as well forget about ever working with each
other again.

The "bone" that they received was a case that involved a larceny of jewelry from a seventy-four-year-old woman on the east side of their city. The police report showed that the crimes had been committed in broad daylight and that the perpetrators had been youthful. This was all the information that was presented to them.

They decided to visit the elderly lady in her home. Before she came to the door, Mrs. X peered nervously out the front window, from behind the drapes. She opened the door just a little and asked, "Yes? What is it?"

Showing her their badges, OC and CC introduced themselves and assured the old woman that they were there to help her. She opened the door and welcomed them in. They could not get over how frail and poor she looked.

This kind lady, stooped over with arthritis and wearing a dark blue, knitted shawl over her shoulders, seemed barely able to speak or move. *How could anyone steal from this poor soul?* CC wondered.

She motioned them over to the couch. "Please sit down," she said as she took a seat in a nearby rocker. "So many policemen have been here already," she commented. "Have you found out anything yet?"

"No, ma'am," CC responded. "We are still searching for clues. Can you tell us what the robbers looked like?"

"Well, my vision's not too good anymore," she explained. "But I do remember that they were just boys—maybe fifteen or sixteen years of age. One of them was short and chubby, and the other one was tall and thin. They seemed like such nice boys." She sighed.

"I understand, Mrs. X, but how did they gain entrance into your home?" OC asked.

Strands of her yellowish-white hair fell from atop her wrinkled head as she shrugged her shoulders, as if in resignation. "They knocked on my door and asked me if they could use my bathroom, and I thought to myself, such nicely dressed young men, what could be the harm in letting them in? I pointed them to the upstairs bathroom, and they literally ran up the steps as if they couldn't wait one second longer. I felt sorry for them," she went on.

"How long were they upstairs? OC queried.

"Well, I thought for a moment that they seemed to be taking a long time, but I didn't worry about it—at first," she told them while hanging her head and shaking it.

The fragile old lady began to weep, as she continued with her story. "While they were upstairs, they ransacked my bedroom, took two diamond rings that had belonged to my mother, and my husband's wedding band. It was all I had left from my husband's possessions," she sniffed. "He wore that gold ring for forty years. They thanked me so sincerely when they came back downstairs. They seemed like such nice boys." She spoke as if she felt totally betrayed.

"Listen, Mrs. X," OC assured her, "we will apprehend the suspects for you, and we will get your valuables back." OC placed his hand on her shoulder to communicate his concern.

"Oh, thank you, thank you," she cried.

On the way back to the detective bureau, OC and CC discussed the case. "Well, we've committed ourselves to this now," OC pointed out. "We've got to come through for her, but how in the world are we going to solve this case? We have no leads at all!"

A few moments later, another detective walked in and asked CC to get a report out of the files. As he was searching through the file drawer, he found reports that revealed a string of larcenies had been committed on the west side of the city over a period of a few months. He ran back to OC and told him what he discovered.

Eagerly putting their heads together, they searched through each larceny file, poring over them in the hopes of finding additional clues to help them solve this case without delay.

In one hour, they discovered several larcenies committed during the past two months that appeared to have been committed by the same two youths. In each of those reports, the perpetrators were described as boys in their teens—one was short and stocky; the other was tall and thin. Often, they had gained entrance into the homes in much the same way as the young thieves had entered Mrs. X's house.

"We've got a lot more ammunition now," OC proclaimed. Armed with their faith and supplemented with additional facts, they got into their patrol car and started to drive around the city.

"Let's get a couple of containers of coffee to go," CC suggested.

"Okay," OC answered as he pulled into their favorite coffee shop.

After buying the coffee, they drove to their special hilltop spot to pray. Admittedly, they were growing somewhat tired and discouraged. But they had faith that God would guide their paths.

As they headed down the main street of the city, OC, who was driving, turned into a municipal parking lot.

"Look at that guy!" CC pointed toward the rear exit of the lot.

"What guy? There are at least six fellows over there."

"The short, stocky one with the blue jacket," CC answered.

"What about him?"

"I don't know for sure, but he matches the description of our suspect."

OC stopped the car, and they surveyed the group of teens for a few moments.

There is a sixth sense that cops develop over years of experience revealing to them specific behavior patterns of criminal suspects. CC's sixth sense was triggered.

"That's him, OC! That's our man," CC declared.

"We have no proof. How can you say that?"

"Please, OC, just believe me. Drive up to that guy."

OC did as directed and asked the boy to get into the patrol car. They advised him of his rights after he told them he was nineteen years old.

Back at the police department both detectives interviewed him. Within ninety minutes, he had confessed to all of the larcenies.

Twenty minutes after they took his statement, a phone call

from an anonymous informant revealed the identities of three other individuals who had been involved in this string of crimes.

OC and CC had been able to apprehend a total of four individuals who had been responsible for the larcenies committed over a period of two months. They also recovered the woman's rings and a vast array of other valuables that had been stolen from the victims of the other crimes.

The next day OC and CC ascertained the identity of a man in another city who operated as a "fence" (someone who buys and sells stolen merchandise). He had been the "middleman" in the cases they were dealing with in their city. OC and CC went to that other city, and with the aid of a detective there, they raided the home of the fence, and recovered thousands of dollars' worth of stolen merchandise.

Within two days, a case that had kept the detective bureau stumped for months had been spilt wide open.

One of the detectives began to question OC and CC.

"You guys have no experience as detectives at all, and yet you solved this important case. How did you do it?"

OC answered, "We put our faith to work, and it all paid off."

But wilt thou know, O vain man, that faith without works is dead? (James 2:20)

DISPATCH 11

DETOURS

For my thoughts are not your thoughts,
neither are your ways my ways, saith the LORD.
—Isaiah 55:8

"There's an opening in the juvenile bureau, and I would like you to serve there," the mayor began talking to CC. "We are confident in your ability to handle these problems because you have proven yourself as a detective."

"Thank you, sir," he responded. "But can OC continue to be my partner?"

"At this time, we have only one slot open for the juvenile bureau, but we'll keep your request in mind."

"Okay, your honor. I really appreciate that. OC and I work well together, and that kind of teamwork really pays off."

"Yes, you and OC have formed a good—and very successful—team. Please understand that these new assignments are based upon the department's present needs."

"I do understand, and I accept this new challenge with gratitude. Thank you very much," said CC.

Working with young people has always inspired CC, and this new opportunity gave him several exciting possibilities. The joy was tempered, however, by the realization that OC and he would not be working together.

"How did your meeting with the mayor go?" OC asked when CC returned to the bureau.

"Okay," he answered. "But I'm afraid I have some bad news."

"What's the matter?"

"I've been assigned to the juvenile bureau."

"That's great! I know how much you like to work with kids."

"Yeah, but I'm so disappointed that we won't be partners any longer."

"Me too, but remember that wonderful promise of God: "And we know that all things work together for good to them that love God, to them who are the called according to his purpose" (Romans 8:28).

For several months, OC and CC had been used by God to help straighten out troubled lives.

Both detectives rededicated their badges to God. "Lord, although we do not understand the present circumstances, we do trust you to help us grow as a result of these changes. You, Lord—not our circumstances or our experiences—are our Lord and Master. We love you and praise you!"

That powerful, life-changing voice that had reverberated within their spirits so many times before spoke to their hearts once more. "Trust in the Lord with all thine heart; and lean not unto thine own understanding" (Proverbs 3:5). They accepted the present circumstances as being God's will.

CC cleared his desk, shook OC's hand, and wished him well. He was ready to embark on a wholly new adventure.

Within four months of his start as a juvenile bureau detective, CC had organized sports programs for every teen who wished to participate. He found that a grouping of teens from well-structured environments with teens who came from troubled homes had a great impact on the overall goal of the program.

The troubled teens could see the value of living more wholesome lives as they interacted with other young people outside of their normal environment. More than 750 teens participated in these programs, and many of them reported that this experience had turned their lives around. It was the first such program that the police department had ever sponsored. The effort also helped to change young people's views of police officers in that it allowed cops and kids to work hand in hand for mutual goals.

Six months after this program developed, the juvenile crime rate had decreased significantly. Hundreds of young people would visit the juvenile bureau offices just to say hello. Many teens, from all backgrounds, became friends of the police. A new sense of pride evolved in the city—among both the kids and the cops.

Before long, judges, journalists, lawyers, and doctors, plus hundreds of other city citizens, expressed their support for these programs. Through all of this, with the help of local clergy, God was glorified. Many young people who had been written off as hopeless cases were experiencing total transformation through faith-based programs that included the teaching of Jesus Christ. Interestingly, very few, if any, parents objected to the spiritual approach in getting through to their kids. In fact, many parents welcomed it.

Dozens of letters, expressing the appreciation of parents, professionals, and city leaders, poured into the police department offices.

When CC first started this program, he was told that he was wasting his time. "These kids can never be straightened out," one hardened officer told him. But CC firmly believed that when we put our faith into action, every doubter would be proven wrong.

One parent went so far as to say, "My son is such a waste!"

"Look," CC said, "if we can succeed in changing your son into a productive person, will you change your attitude and cooperate with what I recommend?"

The father laughed sarcastically but reluctantly agreed.

The very next day, CC placed this man's son (who was addicted to alcohol and drugs) in charge of one of the largest programs. Within two months, he was on his way to getting cured of his drug-dependency problems!

Several months later, his father appeared in the doorway of CC's office. "Thank you, thank you," he cried as the tears streamed down his face. "You have turned my son's life around."

"What do you think caused this change?" CC asked.

With great seriousness on his face, the father replied, "His belief in Jesus Christ."

This was one story among hundreds in which God had taken a family off the road to destruction and placed it on the road to salvation. This father's genuine gratitude filled CC with joy.

Many families, CC discovered, were at the ends of their ropes. Such circumstances, however, enabled these folks to allow God to put their lives and their relationships back together.

Some police officials expressed intense opposition to CC's methods and his programs. The actual statistics of changed lives always countered their arguments, however. One well-known state judge personally commended CC for the work he was doing.

Throughout a one-year period he continued to contact OC, expressing hope that they might be reunited as partners.

"It looks kind of hopeless at this point," OC stated. "But let's continue to pray."

"Prayer changes things." CC echoed, "and let's remember what the Bible says: 'Rejoice evermore' (1 Thessalonians 5:16). 'In everything give thanks; for this is the will of God in Christ Jesus concerning you' (1 Thessalonians 5:18)."

With each new day CC saw more and more people who had been touched by God, and their lives had been straightened out through the power of His Word.

For the word of God is quick, and powerful, and sharper than any two edged sword, piercing even to the dividing asunder of soul and spirit, and of the joints and marrow, and is a discerner of the thoughts and intents of the heart. (Hebrews 4:12)

DISPATCH 12

LESSONS FROM THE SCHOOL OF PRAYER

The effectual fervent prayer of a righteous man availeth much.
—James 5:16

"CC, you will never have to worry about leaving the juvenile bureau; you have done such a good job that you will be here until you retire," a high-ranking police official told him.

Such words should have encouraged him, but they had the effect of disheartening him because he was still hoping and praying to be able to work with OC once again.

He soon discovered that OC's faith concerning this prayer request was weakening at a faster rate than his own. For this reason, he decided not to tell OC about the police official's remarks to him.

Both had found working together to be a golden opportunity to bring change to people's lives. The Word of God, he discovered, has the power to effect social changes.

People who had little knowledge of the power of God were sometimes critical of their methods, but they were always amazed by the results. In fact, some of the family members of their biggest critics sometimes contacted them for spiritual help. They never "talked religion" to people; they only talked God. And they never forced their views on anyone. If someone did not want to listen to them, that was okay. They stopped and discussed solving problems from a secular point of view.

OC and CC got together for coffee one evening. CC picked OC up and drove off to the hilltop where they had dedicated their gold badges to the Lord—their "prayer mountain." They discussed the seemingly impossible odds against them ever being in partnership again. There did seem to be insurmountable obstacles against it—manpower cuts, budget cuts, and other factors. For many months they had prayed about this, but nothing had changed. Yet!

On an unusually warm prespring afternoon, CC received a call from his boss.

"CC," he boomed, "I want you to come into my office. We need to discuss a request I received from the mayor's office."

"Yes, sir," CC replied. "I'll be right over!"

As CC entered the chief's office, he was astounded to see OC sitting in a chair next to his desk.

The boss entered the room, and said, "Thank you for coming over so quickly, men. I wanted to let you know that our city has received a $22,000 grant to organize a crime-prevention program. After reviewing all the personnel files, the mayor has picked you two to set up the program."

Both sat in stunned silence as the chief went on. "Beginning next week, you will work together as a team. Also, you will be going to a southern state next month in order to attend crime prevention school. Congratulations, OC. Congratulations, CC." The chief shook their hands and walked out.

"Jesus answered our prayer," OC! shouted.

"I can't believe it. A $22,000 grant is getting us back together," OC replied.

"God is so good to us. He is such a great God!" said CC.

Without saying anything further, OC and CC knew exactly what they had to do next. Immediately, they drove off to their "prayer mountain" to express their gratitude to God.

They opened a Bible they kept in their car and read, "My

brethren, count it all joy when ye fall into divers temptations; knowing this, that the trying of your faith worketh patience" (James 1:2–3).

God's clear and simple answer should have been obvious to them during the two years they prayed. They had prayed for an instant answer, but God had shown them that His timing is perfect. They had learned two lessons in the school of prayer—to pray without ceasing and to wait patiently. "Pray without ceasing" (1 Thessalonians 5:17). "Wait on the LORD: be of good courage, and he shall strengthen thine heart: wait, I say, on the LORD" (Psalm 27:14). These lessons would not be forgotten.

DISPATCH 13

AMBASSADORS

Now then we are ambassadors for Christ, as
though God did beseech you by us: we pray you
in Christ's stead, be ye reconciled to God.
—2 Corinthians 5:20

OC and CC registered for their required training at a school in the Southeast. Little did they realize that God would use them for a higher purpose—a purpose that altered the course of their lives and the lives of others.

Three weeks before they were scheduled to attend the classes, their boss asked OC to call the school in order to make certain that everything was arranged.

Surprisingly, the receptionist at the school informed OC that the classes they were supposed to attend had been canceled.

"Why were they canceled?" OC inquired.

The young lady answered, "I don't know the reason for it being canceled so abruptly; this has never happened before."

OC and CC were puzzled by this strange alteration of their plans. OC did not respond; he just sat at his desk pensively and stared out the office window.

Just then, their boss reentered the room; "Everything in order for school?" he inquired.

"No," OC answered. "The classes have been canceled."

"Well, we're not going to let that stop us," he announced. The boss got on the phone and began to call other crime prevention schools around the country. "We can't lose that grant," he said with increasing determination.

For two hours they went from one disappointment to the next as each state's crime prevention department said that they had no training facilities for out-of-state cops.

CC was reminded of the important lesson in patience he had recently received. *There is a purpose in all of this*, he thought.

> And we know that all things work together for good
> to them that love God, to them who are the called
> according to his purpose. (Romans 8:28)

By this time, OC was making the calls. He had come to the last school on the list. Before dialing, he looked up at CC and said, "If this next school doesn't have a class for us, the program ends."

OC made the call and asked the receptionist if there were any openings for their spring course in crime prevention training.

"I'm sure that all the classes are filled, sir. But please hold on; I'll check."

Several minutes passed, and both cops were reaching the point where they could hardly bear the suspense. What a disappointment it would be if there were no vacancies at this school.

Finally, the receptionist said, breaking the suspenseful silence, "You guys are very lucky. Two individuals just dropped out of the course, and this gives us openings for you."

For a reason unknown to them at the time, it appeared that the Holy Spirit was leading them to travel to the Midwest instead of the Southeast.

For all who are being led by the Spirit of God, these are sons of God. (Romans 8:14)

The lessons they had recently learned in the school of prayer had to be tested once again, but through this experience they learned to trust God even more.

Trust in the Lord with all thine heart; and lean not unto thine own understanding, In all thy ways acknowledge him, and he shall direct thy paths. (Proverbs 3:5–6)

They had less than two weeks to prepare for a journey that became one of the most incredible experiences of their lives.

On a cool Monday morning they boarded a 727 jet and soon took off for the school they would be attending.

While OC gazed out the window at the billowy, white clouds that seemed to form a cushion beneath them, CC began to read a book about prayer. Out of the corner of his eye, he could see that the screaming roar of the jet engines and the turbulence in the air were making OC a bit nervous. He was gripping the arms of his seat, with white knuckles showing, as if he was holding on for dear life.

"I've never flown in a jet before," he told CC, after he kidded him about his nervousness.

"Don't worry, OC, you will be fine," CC assured him.

"You know, CC, before I left my house, I prayed about how many pocket New Testaments I should bring on this trip to distribute in Texas."

"How many did you bring?" CC asked.

"Well, I felt that I was being led to take seven, but that was all I had at home, so I only brought five. Now I feel guilty because if I encounter seven people in Texas who need the Testaments, I won't be able to give them to two people," OC replied.

"That's a confirmation, OC. I also prayed about how many New Testaments to take with me, and I was led to bring two. Five plus two is seven! Now that is interesting."

Sitting on the other side of CC (the seats were three abreast on both sides of the aisle), was a young man named K with whom he was talking.

CC felt an inner urging to tell K about the Lord. He was a pleasant man of about thirty years old. "Lord," CC prayed silently, "please give me an opening to share the good news with K." CC felt certain that this man was the first of the seven people whom God had numbered to receive the Testaments.

Before long, K began to open up to CC about some of his personal struggles. "I am the most qualified person for my job, and I have the most seniority, and yet each time a promotion is given out, it always goes to a lesser-qualified individual. It's at the point where I feel like quitting my job."

This openness on K's part enabled CC to share with him how he had received his promotion in the police department.

"For a long time, I kept praying, and I believed in faith that I would receive an answer but understanding that if it was not God's will, I would be okay because He had something better for me," said CC.

> "Saying, Father, if thou be willing, remove this cup from me: nevertheless, not my will, but thine, be done." (Luke 22:42)

K listened politely with an obvious degree of curiosity, if not personal interest.

"The only way you can possibly achieve success is through Jesus Christ," CC explained. Then he handed him a New Testament. "Thank you," K responded.

No conversation passed between them from that point on, and

the only sound to be heard was the rustling of pages as K flipped through his pocket Testament.

CC glanced at K a few times, and he could see that he was intensely involved in reading. OC and CC kept K in prayer while he was reading. They asked God to open his eyes to spiritual truth.

The pilot announced over the intercom system, "Ladies and gentlemen, please fasten your seat belts. We will be approaching the airport in fifteen minutes."

They all fastened their seat belts and then K turned to OC, handing the New Testament back to him. "Thank you," he said again.

Looking directly into K's eyes, OC said, "Please keep it, it is a gift from Jesus. He used us as His ambassadors to deliver His Word to you."

> Now then we are ambassadors for Christ, as though God did beseech you by us: we pray you in Christ's stead, be ye reconciled to God. (2 Corinthians 5:20)

K clutched the little book close to his chest and explained, "You know, I've always wanted to read the Bible, but I never seemed to be able to find the time because I was so busy. I guess I needed your helping hands."

As they got up to disembark, OC and CC shook hands with K. "Remember, friend," CC said, "if you want peace, success, and personal blessings, you can find them only in a personal relationship with Jesus Christ."

> "Peace I leave with you, my peace I give unto you: not as the world giveth, give I unto you. Let not your heart be troubled, neither let it be afraid." (John 14:27)

Both cops prayed a blessing on K, and he looked up with tears in his eyes. "May God bless you both," he said as they walked toward the exit.

"Remember, K, Christians don't have to say goodbye. We can say 'see you later' because we will see each other again—in heaven," said CC.

One Bible gone and six to go OC thought as they boarded another flight to their final destination.

DISPATCH 14

A QUESTION THAT SHOOK A SOUL

According to the eternal purpose which he purposed
in Christ Jesus our Lord: In whom we have boldness
and access with confidence by the faith of him.
—Ephesians 3:11–12

After arriving at the airport at the designated time, the cops met a guide who took them to a hotel approximately forty miles away, in a small city where the school was located.

As soon as they registered in the hotel, they realized what a busy schedule lay ahead. The classes would be conducted in the hotel—eight to nine hours per day. They would also have all their meals in the hotel dining room.

"Well, it looks like we're not going to get in much sightseeing," CC said with a laugh, turning to OC.

"Nope. I wonder what we'll do with all of our spare time," OC countered.

"Even if we had much spare time," OC went on, "it doesn't look like there's a whole lot to do around here." They both laughed heartily.

Some of the other men made remarks about this "god-forsaken place." OC and CC, however, soon learned that God had not forsaken this place in any respect.

After supper on the second evening of their stay in the hotel, OC and CC decided to sit and talk for a while. A waiter, carrying a large tray filled with dirty dishes, walked by their table. Without thinking, CC blurted out to him, "Hey, how's God treating you?"

Stunned, the waiter turned to CC and stared at him. "What do you mean? He treats me good!"

The young waiter placed his tray on a table and sat down with the cops. "Why do you ask me about God?" he asked, somewhat defensively.

"To tell you the truth, I don't even know. I just felt this urge to ask you," CC explained. "What's your name?"

"I'm YP."

As this conversation began to warm up, OC and CC learned that YP was twenty-five years old. He began to ask them freely about their relationship with God. As OC and CC told him about Jesus Christ, YP's eyes flooded with tears.

"What brings you here?" YP asked.

"Well," OC explained, "we are cops who were supposed to attend training classes in another state, but those classes were canceled, and we believe that God led us here, to meet people like you."

"That's really something, man," YP responded with increasing interest. "If ever I needed to talk to someone it is now. For several years I have been searching, but I don't know what for. I've bounced around from job to job, never finding fulfillment in my work—or my life. It seems like life is so empty—so meaningless. Finally— about two years ago—I called out to God for help."

"YP!" a woman's voice yelled from the kitchen. He jumped up and politely excused himself, carrying the dishes hurriedly back to the kitchen.

OC and CC were left in total amazement over their encounter with YP. It was incomprehensible to realize that God had used them to deliver His message to this young man who had prayed for over two years for God to answer his prayer.

Both cops retired to their room. At about 8:00 p.m. they heard a knock at their door. OC opened the door—YP was there with two of his young friends.

"Would you please tell my two friends about Jesus Christ?"

"Sure, YP," OC responded. "Please come in."

For more than one hour OC and CC shared Jesus with YP and his two friends. Their eyes burned with joy, innocence, and curiosity. It was such a joy to minister to them.

Before long, all three of them had given their hearts and lives to Jesus Christ. OC gave each of them a pocket New Testament and told them it would be their guide in the days ahead.

"Thank you," they all said.

"You are welcome," CC responded.

On his way out the door, YP said, "My heart burns with a desire to tell all my friends about Jesus Christ!"

The young man's countenance had changed from an angry, distrustful scowl to a happy, peaceful glow that radiated the love of Jesus Christ.

> "Peace I leave with you, my peace I give unto you: not as the world giveth, give I unto you. Let not your heart be troubled, neither let it be afraid." (John 14:27)

DISPATCH 15

SHARPER THAN A TWO-EDGED SWORD

For the word of God is alive and exerts power and
is sharper than any two-edged sword and pierces
even to the dividing of soul and spirit.
—Hebrews 4:12

Usually after supper OC and CC would take a long walk through
the countryside. CC wasn't feeling well on this evening, so he
decided to go back to the hotel room for a nap. OC told him that
he would walk down to a park—a shortcut to the hotel. "I'll return
within two hours."

The park was beautifully lighted. It was a balmy evening, and
his walk was most enjoyable. He strolled through some woods, past
a couple of quiet ponds, and finally approached a large building that
he discovered to be a music arts building. The structure was round,
and it was surrounded by a moat. He went over a little bridge and
approached the entrance, thinking that he might be able to attend
an interesting concert or another event. While he approached the
entrance, he came face to face with a young lady and young man,
both in their twenties.

"Do you know if any special musical programs are taking place
tonight?" CC asked.

The young lady answered no, and all three began to converse about several subjects—all small talk.

At one point, CC said something to the effect about God's creation of trees, grass, and other natural beauties.

Suddenly, the young lady looked at CC and said, "There is no god! I used to pray to a so-called god, who was supposed to be in a place called heaven." She gestured to the sky. "But I found out it's all nonsense. When he didn't hear my prayers, I decided to live my life the way I wanted to. If there is a God, I want him to speak directly to me. I want to hear his words," she said in a defiant manner. The young man, although listening politely, said nothing.

CC now had the opening he was waiting for and explained to the young woman and man that he believed it was no accident that they encountered each other. He began to speak to them about hope in Christ.

> Now the God of hope fill you with all joy and peace
> in believing, that ye may abound in hope, through
> the power of the Holy Ghost. (Romans 15:13)

After about a half hour of speaking, the young woman suddenly said, "I like what you are saying. I will try God. What do I have to lose?"

After speaking for a few more minutes, CC said to both the young woman and man, "I would like you to meet my friend OC, who can answer any questions you might have."

When they met OC, he gave the young woman the fifth pocket New Testament he had and shared some verses and instructed her to read it daily.

"Thank you both so much; I am glad I met both of you," she said as she and her friend were ready to leave. "I will never forget this experience."

"Always remember that Jesus will never leave you; He will always be by your side. God bless you," CC admonished.

> Let your conversation be without covetousness; and be content with such things as ye have: for he hath said, I will never leave thee, nor forsake thee. (Hebrews 13:5)

As OC and CC were returning to their hotel, they noticed dozens of people wading in a pond.

OC and CC sat down on a bench overlooking the pond. "Wouldn't it be great to be able to tell all these people about Jesus?" he mentioned.

"Yes. You know, I'll bet many of them are going through the same kind of misery that young woman experienced."

At that same moment, a young man came over and sat down next to them. He was trembling. "Boy, am I in trouble," he said, shaking his head.

"What kind of trouble?" CC asked.

"My life is a living nightmare. I've committed every sin there is—drugs, stealing. You name it, and I've done it!"

"You really feel bad, don't you?" OC asked.

"Man, I've sunk so low that I must be just dirt to God. He could never forgive me for all I've done."

CC interrupted him. "What's your name?"

"I don't want to tell you," he replied. His posture and all his mannerisms showed that he was severely depressed.

"Listen to me. Look at all the benches where you could have chosen to sit down. Yet you came to sit by us. That was no accident. I believe that God led you here," CC told him.

OC interjected, "Jesus came to earth nearly two thousand years ago to die for our sins. That was why He was nailed to the cross—to take away your sins."

"Even mine?" he asked, revealing a spark of interest.

"Yes," CC continued. "No matter what you've done, God can forgive you. He wants to, and He can do it right now."

With his mouth wide open and tears brimming in his eyes, this young man asked, "Do you think God will take my sins away and give me a fresh start?"

"Jesus will forgive you. He will give you a new reason for living and guide you throughout your life if you accept Him as your personal Savior and friend."

Both cops carefully led him through the steps of salvation and the sinner's prayer.

After praying together, he jumped up, hugged both, and thanked them profusely for leading him to Jesus. They gave him the sixth New Testament and encouraged him to keep on with his new Christian life.

"You know, OC," CC said, "this is like being an obstetrician. It's so great to be used by God to usher in a new birth. He prepares each person's heart to receive the good news, and it's our job to bring them through to spiritual rebirth. I have never met anyone who was so ready to receive Jesus, and I wonder what would have happened to that guy if we had not been there on that bench."

The cops looked at each other in amazement. "It is an adventure to be led by the Spirit of God," OC said.

"Yes," CC replied. "I wonder who number seven will be?"

DISPATCH 16

MISSION ACCOMPLISHED

Seek ye first the kingdom of God, and his righteousness
and all these things shall be added unto you.
—Matthew 6:33

It was to be their final day at school. They had gone through the crime prevention course successfully and had their graduation the night before. It had been announced at the ceremonies that OC had ended the course at the top of the class. CC was proud of him and was honored to be his friend and partner.

The beautiful sun was beginning to rise on this Sunday morning. While lying on his bed, CC began to flip through the pages of the local telephone directory when his eyes fell upon a church address.

"Hey, OC, let's go to church!"

"Where?" he called back.

"There's a church in the city, their service starts at ten thirty."

"Okay, I'm with you," he answered.

After breakfast, they rented a car and went off to look for the church. They discovered, to their surprise, that it was only one mile away.

They found the little, white frame building on the outskirts of the city—a beautiful country church. They parked the car and went to look for the pastor.

A few moments later they met a young, enthusiastic man who seemed so full of the Spirit of the Lord. "Good morning. I'm Pastor Q. Welcome to our church."

After they introduced themselves and explained their background to the pastor, as well as their testimony of what occurred during their stay, the pastor invited them to lead the entire morning worship service and to share their testimony with the congregation. OC and CC's hearts rejoiced at this opportunity.

About fifty people attended the service. There were farmers in overalls, businessmen in suits, and many happy, active children. It was such a warm group of people.

After the pastor introduced them to his congregation, they began to minister to these beautiful people. As OC and CC shared their testimonies, they noticed some of the people take cloths from their pockets to wipe away their tears.

Just as the service ended, the pastor asked OC and CC to come over to where he was standing and asked the entire congregation to rise and pray for both.

Everyone was in tears. God had clearly spoken. OC and CC had gone to the church to get encouragement, but they ended up encouraging the congregation.

They bade farewell to the pastor and his people, feeling completely revitalized for their return trip home.

Two hours later they were bound for home. They thanked God all the way home for all He had done for them and through them.

When their jet landed, they got into an unmarked police car that was waiting for them. It was driven by one of the detectives.

As they headed toward the police station, OC opened his briefcase. "Hey, CC, look. I still have one New Testament left. Do you think we forgot someone?"

Before CC could answer him, the detective driving turned

around and said, "They just hired a new guy to work with both of you. He reports to work tomorrow."

CC looked at OC. "Hold onto that Bible, partner. We didn't forget anyone. That Bible is marked for the new guy."

A FINAL WORD FROM THE LIEUTENANT

Now more than ever, cops need to hear words they can trust. Not empty words from people who cannot be trusted, but truthful words that can be found in only one book—the Holy Bible!

One day while reading in the book of Romans, I came across these verses:

> Obey the government, for God is the one who has put it there. There is no government anywhere that God has not placed in power. So those who refuse to obey the laws of the land are refusing to obey God, and punishment will follow. For the policeman does not frighten people who are doing right; but those doing evil will always fear him. So, if you don't want to be afraid, keep the laws and you will get along well. The policeman is sent by God to help you. But if you are doing something wrong, of course you should be afraid, for he will have you punished. He is sent by God for that very purpose. Obey the laws, then, for two reasons: first, to keep from being punished, and second, just because you know you should. (Romans 13:3–4 TLB)

Through these verses, I came to understand that being a cop is a sacred calling. This reality became a spark that ignited within my spirit to get this message about Christ to my fellow cops and their families. A message I came to realize would be life changing for them.

This burning passion became my goal in life. Far too many of my fellow cops had fallen prey to the temptations that are peculiar to their careers. Today's cop is sometimes particularly vulnerable to the ravages of alcoholism, drug abuse, broken marriages, extramarital affairs, mental illness, and other problems. Some of this may be due to the breakdown of traditional values in our society. It seems, for example, that cops often receive little respect from our citizens, and this factor, along with long absences from home, shift work, and the hazardous nature of police work, often hinders the individual cop's success in life.

Many cops I know lost their marriage relationships, their families, their health, and, sadly, their lives, as a result of suicide because, in their view, they had no one to turn to for help.

I know that life teachings of Jesus Christ would be a great help to my colleagues in law enforcement. The Word of God is indeed a trusted Word.

> For unto us a child is born, unto us a son is given: and the government shall be upon his shoulder: and his name shall be called Wonderful, Counsellor, The mighty God, The everlasting Father, The Prince of Peace. (Isaiah 9:6)

It has been a great privilege for me to be able to share this story of how two cops and God become close brothers in blue.—Lieutenant Franklin Philip

PART 3

SURVIVAL GUIDE FOR THE TWENTY-FIRST CENTURY CENTURION

Note: Cops in biblical times were known as centurions.

ROLL CALL

So then every one of us shall give account of himself to God.
—Romans 14:12

This survival guide will bring you comfort from God's Word, unity with God's Spirit, and peace from God's heart.

May the words you read on each page of this book fill your heart with hope, your faith with strength, and your life with the peace of our Lord Jesus Christ as you serve to enforce the laws of man and the laws of God.

From time to time you will face difficulties on the job and troubles at home, which can become overwhelming. When this happens, you will find this survival guide to be a shining light during your darkest hours.

The Lord has a special place in his heart for you. As you patrol the streets of your city, our highways, walk the prison halls keeping a close eye on criminals, or perform whatever task you have, spend some time and ponder on the things of God, for He will lead you to safer places during your life's journey.

When trials and tribulations come your way, never forget that Jesus has a shoulder for you to lean on, ears willing to listen to your pleas for help, and arms strong enough to hold you up during your weakest moments.

Jesus is a partner who will stand by your side "in the heat of fire" and stand in front of you as a protective shield when you are "under fire."

May the words in this survival guide bring healing to your

broken heart, warmth to dry your precious tears, encouragement to lift your spirit, and the reality of the profound truth that Christ is a true brother in blue.

—Lieutenant Franklin Philip

TWO HISTORICAL ENCOUNTERS BETWEEN COPS AND GOD

And he said O Lord God of my master Abraham,
I pray thee, send me good speed this day, and
shew kindness unto my master Abraham.
—Genesis 24:12

I believe that the first "cop" to have an encounter with Jesus Christ was a Roman named Cornelius. (Enforcers of the law were referred to as centurions in early biblical times.) We can look at him as a "police chief" of his time who worked in the city of Caesarea during early New Testament days. He was well-known throughout his region as being an honest man who was devoted to his job, his family, and God.

Cornelius was the first gentile to convert to Christianity after hearing the apostle Peter preaching in the streets near his home. "There was a certain man in Caesarea called Cornelius, a centurion of the band called the Italian band, A devout man, and one that feared God with all his house, which gave much alms to the people, and prayed to God always" (Acts 10:1–2).

Another encounter between Christ and a "cop" is recorded in the book of Matthew, chapter 8. Here we read about a cop asking Christ to heal his ill and suffering servant.

When Jesus agreed to heal this man's servant, he (the cop) told Christ that he did not deserve God's blessing. He knew that all Christ had to do was to say the word, and his servant would be healed.

"Wherefore neither thought I worthy to come unto thee: but say in a word, and my servant shall be healed. For I also am a man set under authority, having under me soldiers, and I say unto one, Go, and he goeth; and to another, Come, and he cometh; and to my servant, Do this, and he doeth it. When Jesus heard these things, he marvelled at him, and turned him about, and said unto the people that followed him, I say unto you, I have not found so great faith, no, not in Israel" (Luke 7:8–9).

As Jesus spoke to these Roman "cops," he speaks to you at this hour. He is ready, willing, and able to help you right now. "That ye put off concerning the former conversation the old man, which is corrupt according to the deceitful lusts; And be renewed in the spirit of your mind; And that ye put on the new man, which after God is created in righteousness and true holiness" (Ephesians 4:22, 23, 24).

COPS AND ANXIETY

You will experience many emotions during your entire career. This emotional roller coaster can bring on stress and affect your physical and mental well-being. When things become overwhelming for you to cope with, take some time and read this wonderful scripture: "Be careful for nothing; but in everything by prayer and supplication with thanksgiving let your requests be made known unto God. And the peace of God, which passeth all understanding, shall keep your hearts and minds through Christ Jesus" (Philippians 4:6–7).

The longer you focus on your troubles, the bigger they get;
the longer you focus on Christ, the bigger He gets.

COPS AND ANGER

All of us become angry from time to time. It's how we handle our anger that challenges our character. There is something called "righteous anger." It is not a sin to get angry over a legitimate matter, but don't let your anger boil over to a sinful act.

Out-of-control anger will not do you any good and will not please God. When you are confronted with a situation which can cause you to become angry, take a deep breath, keep cool, and remember that what you say today in anger has the potential to leave you and others with deep scars tomorrow. "He that is slow to anger is better than the mighty; and he that ruleth his spirit than he that taketh a city" (Proverbs 16:32).

COPS AND ASKING FOR HELP

Many cops are facing difficult times on the job and at home and yet never ask for help. I am sure this is common in all police departments. When many cops go through a difficult time, they hesitate to ask for help.

Know this! You can do three things to get the spiritual help you need when you need it: you can *ask* God for guidance; you can *seek* God's intervention; you can *knock* at His door via the Bible and find the guidance you need during your most difficult times. "Ask, and it shall be given you; seek, and ye shall find; knock, and it shall be opened unto you" (Matthew 7:7).

Cops and Walking the Beat, Standing Post, Patrolling the Streets

Do not walk, stand, or sit with individuals who will lead you away from what is right in the eyes of God. Instead, walk with God, stand on God's word, and sit with people who will be a blessing to you.

Many times, cops are put in positions that could very well compromise their oath of office when associating with bad people, especially bad cops. Doctoring a police report, lying about an incident, covering up for a fellow officer who committed an unlawful or unethical act can happen during a time when you are walking, standing, or sitting with someone who cares nothing about *you* but only about themselves.

> Blessed is the man that walketh not in the counsel
> of the ungodly, nor standeth in the way of sinners,
> nor sitteth in the seat of the scornful. But his delight
> is in the law of the Lord; and in his law doth he
> meditate day and night. And he shall be like a tree
> planted by the rivers of water, that bringeth forth his
> fruit in his season; his leaf also shall not wither; and
> whatsoever he doeth shall prosper. (Psalm 1:1–3)

Living by these principles will prevent a lot of misery and pain in your life. You will find mercy and grace from God when you most need them.

Cops and Trust

Cops generally do not trust many people. However, the one person you can trust is *God*! When you seek His guidance, He will answer. Why not have your next cup of coffee with Him who sits in the Heavens above and learn how trustworthy He is.

Hear me when I call, O God of my righteousness: thou hast enlarged me when I was in distress; have mercy upon me, and hear my prayer. (Psalm 4:1)

Give ear to my prayer, O God; and hide not thyself from my supplication. (Psalm 55:1)

Evening, and morning, and at noon, will I pray, and cry aloud, and he shall hear my voice. (Psalm 55:17)

Though he slay me, yet will I trust in him: but I will maintain mine own ways before him. (Job 13:15)

COPS AND REACTIVE VS. PROACTIVE POLICING

It is important for you to know and understand federal, state, and local laws as well as patrol tactics to effectively perform your duties.

Police traditionally have employed reactive policing methodologies. Meaning, their primary focus is to respond to a crime after the fact.

Throughout the history of law enforcement, we have found that the most effective police patrol tactic is proactive policing. This patrol procedure is designed to prevent crime before it occurs.

Most of us live our lives in a "reactive policing" mode. We go along our merry way, not thinking of the consequences our words or actions have on ourselves or others, and then when we find our words and actions get us into trouble—*damage control!*

I am convinced that the Bible offers all of us a "proactive policing" plan for our lives. A plan to help prevent us from the dangers of life.

The entire proactive plan God offers us is in the book of Proverbs. There are thirty-one proverbs, one for each day of the week. Read a chapter in the book of Proverbs each day, and watch how God will work in your life.

> Wisdom is the principal thing; therefore get wisdom: and with all thy getting get understanding. (Proverbs 4:7)

COPS AND ENCOURAGEMENT

Each day that cops report for duty they encounter many people who have nothing positive to say and who make a living at criticizing the police. In fact, police work has become known as a thankless job.

But let not your heart be troubled. Be encouraged and inspired by God's promises. He does not forget the good you do for people. Blessings to you are His reward for the duty you perform.

> For God is not unrighteous to forget your work and labour of love, which ye have shewed toward his name, in that ye have ministered to the saints, and do minister. (Hebrews 6:10)

> My help cometh from the Lord, which made heaven and earth. (Psalm 121:2)

COPS AND THE *L* WORD

Many of us don't talk about love as quite often as we should. Nevertheless, we all need love. God's love for you is unconditional. When you feel unloved, alone, and depressed, remember these promises from Him who sits in the Heavens.

Because he hath set his love upon me, therefore will I deliver him: I will set him on high, because he hath known my name. (Psalm 91:14)

For God so loved the world, that he gave his only begotten Son, that whosoever believeth in him should not perish, but have everlasting life. (John 3:16)

And Jesus said unto them, I am the bread of life: he that cometh to me shall never hunger; and he that believeth on me shall never thirst. (John 6:35)

COPS AND PRAYER

Cops are called upon to take care of and bring comfort to a multiple number of people in crisis. Many times, it is cops who need care and comfort when they have a crisis of their own. You will find comfort at the cross of Christ. All you need to do is to call out His name and pray. Prayer is the only way to communicate with God. You need not do anything formal when you pray. Simply get alone with God and talk to Him as you would talk to anyone else. That is the sincerest way to pray—from the heart.

Then called I upon the name of the Lord; O Lord, I beseech thee, deliver my soul. (Psalm 116:4)

And the Lord shall guide thee continually, and satisfy thy soul in drought, and make fat thy bones: and thou shalt be like a watered garden, and like a spring of water, whose waters fail not. (Isaiah 58:11)

COPS AND BATHSHEBA

Of all the survival tips in this guide you have read, this one may be the most important.

Throughout my entire career in law enforcement I have seen many cops become victimized by what I call the "Bathsheba effect."

Some cops survive the impending doom brought on by this effect. Others unfortunately, do not survive and see their careers, their families, and their very lives destroyed. Take heed what you are about to read. This may be about *you*!

As an illustration of the "Bathsheba effect" I use the story about a "police chief" (my description) during Old Testament times. His name was David, King David, to be exact. He was the chief law enforcer of his kingdom and was anointed and blessed by God. "And when he had removed him, he raised up unto them David to be their king; to whom also he gave testimony, and said, I have found David the son of Jesse, a man after mine own heart, which shall fulfil all my will" (Acts 13:22).

A tragic turn of events in the life of King David occurred when he chose to stay home in Jerusalem after sending his army into battle.

(This event regarding King David's sinful act is in the book of 2 Samuel, chapter 11).

With David's army away, he has some idle time to relax and decides to take a walk on the palace roof. As he is looking at the landscape of his kingdom, he sees a beautiful woman bathing on her roof.

Instead of ignoring her, he sends a messenger to find out who she is. The messenger returned and told David that her name is Bathsheba, the daughter of Eliam and the wife of Uriah, one of his commanders whom he sent out to battle.

Although he discovered that Bathsheba was married and should have ignored her, David invites her to the palace and sleeps with her.

Several weeks later Bathsheba sent word to David revealing to him that she is pregnant.

This news, David knew, was life changing for him—and not in a good way. He feared that if anyone learned about what he did—commit adultery—there would be serious consequences for him.

The next thing David does is make matters worse by not confessing his sin to God; instead, he attempts to cover up his sinful act by ordering Uriah to return home so that he could spend a night with his wife Bathsheba, thus making her pregnancy look like it came as a result of her time with him.

To David's dismay Uriah refused to sleep with his wife while his troops were off fighting.

In a panic, David decides to do the unthinkable. He sent Uriah back to the battlefield and assigns him to the front lines. David then sends a message to another battlefield commander, ordering him to withdraw his troops and leave Uriah alone in battle. Uriah was killed. Now David, so he thought, was off the hook and married Bathsheba.

Unfortunately for David, he was not off the hook. A prophet named Nathan stopped by the palace to visit him and told him that everything he did regarding his relationship with Bathsheba was witnessed by someone from start to finish. "The eyes of the Lord are in every place, beholding the evil and the good" (Proverbs 15:3).

Nathan told David that he would pay a price for his sin and that the son Bathsheba was expecting would die. And not only did the son die, David nearly lost his kingdom and would have lost his life had he not repented of his sin and restored his fellowship with God.

Quite often I had seen cops and others who I knew were married and lived good lives and followed the rules, lived up to their oath of office and never compromised their faith in God, until *she* came along—"Bathsheba!"

The result for all of them was the same. Every one of these cops who committed this sinful act and failed to repent suffered the same fate as did King David.

God gives all of us a very clear and unmistakable warning in His Word about the consequences of becoming the victim of the "Bathsheba effect."

> For the lips of a strange woman drop as an honeycomb, and her mouth is smoother than oil: But her end is bitter as wormwood, sharp as a two-edged sword. Her feet go down to death; her steps take hold on hell. Lest thou shouldest ponder the path of life, her ways are moveable, that thou canst not know them. Hear me now therefore, O ye children, and depart not from the words of my mouth. Remove thy way far from her, and come not nigh the door of her house: Lest thou give thine honour unto others, and thy years unto the cruel: Lest strangers be filled with thy wealth; and thy labours be in the house of a stranger; And thou mourn at the last, when thy flesh and thy body are consumed, And say, How have I hated instruction, and my heart despised reproof; And have not obeyed the voice of my teachers, nor inclined mine ear to them that instructed me! I was almost in all evil in the midst of the congregation and assembly. Drink waters out of thine own cistern, and running waters out of thine own well. Let thy fountains be dispersed abroad, and rivers of waters in the streets. Let them be only thine own, and not strangers' with thee. Let thy fountain be blessed: and rejoice with the wife of thy youth. Let her be as the loving hind and pleasant roe; let her breasts satisfy thee at all times; and be thou ravished always with her

love. And why wilt thou, my son, be ravished with a strange woman, and embrace the bosom of a stranger? For the ways of man are before the eyes of the Lord, and he pondereth all his goings. His own iniquities shall take the wicked himself, and he shall be holden with the cords of his sins. He shall die without instruction; and in the greatness of his folly he shall go astray. (Proverbs 5:3–23)

COPS AND MARRIAGE

The family is God's most sacred institution. The Bible reveals that the first family, consisting of Adam and Eve, was blessed by God. "And God blessed them, and God said unto them, Be fruitful, and multiply, and replenish the earth, and subdue it: and have dominion over the fish of the sea, and over the fowl of the air, and over every living thing that moveth upon the earth." (Genesis 1:28)

They were God's finest work. He loved them, cared for them, provided for them, and gave them every comfort for a wonderful life. But something terrible happened to this couple.

Instead of being obedient to God, they sinned against Him, and the consequences for their disobedience have affected mankind to this day. "And unto Adam he said, Because thou hast hearkened unto the voice of thy wife, and hast eaten of the tree, of which I commanded thee, saying, Thou shalt not eat of it: cursed is the ground for thy sake; in sorrow shalt thou eat of it all the days of thy life." (Genesis 3:17)

Today, God commands cops not to touch the fruits of sin. But like the serpent that tempted the first family in the Garden of Eden, *you* too will be tempted by a serpent to do something totally contrary to God's law. When you yield to temptation, you begin the fall toward sin, and in time you will feel the pain from the serpent's venom and then plunge directly toward destruction.

You may be tempted toward excessive drinking, adultery, gambling, drugs, etc. Whatever it takes Satan to destroy you and your family, he will try to do it. He will put the "forbidden fruit" in front of you.

If you keep your eyes fixed on Christ, and build your house—that is, your life—on the rock, which is the Word of God, you will be secure. Doing otherwise is to head toward destruction.

> Therefore whosoever heareth these sayings of mine, and doeth them, I will liken him unto a wise man, which built his house upon a rock: And the rain descended, and the floods came, and the winds blew, and beat upon that house; and it fell not: for it was founded upon a rock. And every one that heareth these sayings of mine, and doeth them not, shall be likened unto a foolish man, which built his house upon the sand: And the rain descended, and the floods came, and the winds blew, and beat upon that house; and it fell: and great was the fall of it. (Matthew 7:24–27)

COPS AND TESTIMONY

Testimony is a particularly important function of the cop. Many times, cops are called to testify in a court of law regarding specific criminal cases.

Our faith is built on the testimony of people who have seen God act on their behalf. Don't resist hearing the testimony of others who have seen God in action.

If we receive the witness of men, the witness of God is greater: for this is the witness of God which he hath testified of his Son. (1 John 5:9)

Behold, I stand at the door, and knock: if any man hear my voice, and open the door, I will come in to him, and will sup with him, and he with me. (Revelation 3:20)

So then faith cometh by hearing, and hearing by the word of God. (Romans 10:17)

Cops and the *S* Word

No one likes to talk about the *s* word, especially cops! But many people try to justify their commission of so called "harmless small sins."

It is important for us to clearly understand that no sin is small. If the small sin is not taken care of today, it will become a *big* problem tomorrow. Look at a small hole the size of a pinhead on a car windshield. If not immediately repaired, that pinhole becomes a crack. When the crack shatters, the entire windshield breaks and gives way to destruction. This is exactly how sin works. It is a small thing to the sinner. But sooner or later it becomes a *big* problem for all to see.

Everyone who sins against God eventually gets caught, and they pay a heavy price. If you are a cop in sin, you better read on! There is one of two ways you can get out of your troubles; the cross of Christ—"Jesus saith unto him, I am the way, the truth, and the life: no man cometh unto the Father, but by me" (John 14:6)—, or the stake of death—"The wicked shall be turned into hell, and all the nations that forget God" (Psalm 9:17).

COPS AND REPENTANCE

The way to survive the wrath of sin is through a sincere confession of your sins directly to God. Get alone with God in your patrol car, at your office, at home—anywhere—and tell Him that you want to get your life back in order.

Don't let problems consume your life. Jesus promised that the second you sincerely repent, He will forgive you and put you on a sure road to recovery.

> Come now, and let us reason together, saith the Lord: though your sins be as scarlet, they shall be as white as snow; though they be red like crimson, they shall be as wool. (Isaiah 1:18)

NOW IS THE HOUR TO PATROL THE ROMAN ROAD

That if thou shalt confess with thy mouth the Lord Jesus, and shalt believe in thine heart that God hath raised him from the dead, thou shalt be saved. (Romans 10:9)

Confess with your mouth that Jesus Christ is Lord and believe in your heart that God raised Him from the dead so that your sins may be forgiven. It is as simple as that!

A COP'S FINAL TESTIMONY BEFORE HIS/HER FINAL ROLL CALL

Lord God, I confess that I am a sinner. At times I have made a mess of things. I admit that I can't do this alone anymore. I am coming to you, letting you know from my heart that I truly believe Jesus came to this earth, shed his blood, and rose from the dead so that every sin I have ever committed may be forgiven. I believe that Jesus sits at the right hand of the Father and that one day we will meet. I now accept Jesus Christ as my personal Lord, Savior, and Master. Amen

Sign your name here _____

Date_____

Keep this new "birth certificate" for the rest of your life!